I0731347

FILTHY DEAL

DIRTY MAFIA GAMES

MIKA LANE

HEADLANDS PUBLISHING

COPYRIGHT

Copyright© 2020 by Mika Lane
Headlands Publishing
4200 Park Blvd. #244
Oakland, CA 94602

BE THE FIRST TO KNOW...

Want more heat, heart,
and bad boys who know what they're doing?
Join my list and I'll send the steam straight to your inbox,
starting with a deliciously naughty story:

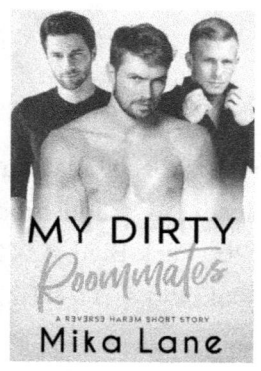

RAIN

"ROUGH NIGHT?"

Well.

A good-looking guy in Las Vegas.

I was beginning to think they were all soft and pasty and wore Members Only jackets. Like all the other guys surrounding me in the elevator.

He looked from the strappy heels dangling from my fingers, to my feet.

Yes, I was walking around a Las Vegas hotel barefoot.

At least my pedi rocked.

At the time I thought it had been a rough night. Turned out I didn't know the half of it.

"Yeah. I needed a break from these torture devices," I said, waving them around. He had no idea how much women suffered wearing these goddamn things. Men should wear heels for a day. See how *they* liked it.

Amusement lit his face, and he stared at me for a moment, leaving me squirming.

Sensing my discomfort, he looked away. Out of the corner of my eye, I could see him looking at the floor, pressing his lips together and trying not to laugh.

Damn, this was a slow elevator. But then, The Venetian's elevators were always slow. Great hotel for the price, but it was starting to show its age. Of course, it didn't help that people were getting off on *every floor*.

And it was three in the goddamn morning. But that was Las Vegas for you. No windows, endless bright lights, and lots of food and alcohol available around the clock. Even the outdoor swimming pools were so brightly lit you wouldn't know it was the middle of the night unless you spotted the moon.

Yeah, Vegas was the land of the twenty-four-hour lifestyle. There was little nine-to-fiving going on here. Just ask my sister, Mazzy.

At the witching hour of three a.m., she was up in our room—yes, the room we were supposedly sharing —boning some stranger.

And because of that, I was *not* in bed, sleeping—the one place in the world I really wanted to be.

I was tired. I was not happy.

And my feet were screaming in pain.

But I'd nonetheless grabbed my shoes and bag when she came blasting in with her booty call, just as I'd been brushing my teeth, getting ready to crash after a long night of pretending I was having fun partying it up in Vegas. I needed to get a little beauty sleep in preparation for the next day's strenuous plan to sit by the pool and soak up rays. So much for that. All I could hope for at this point was to sit by the pool and catch a nap.

Mazzy's booty call was an Uber driver, the very one who'd dropped us in front of the hotel not long before I'd found myself in a crowded elevator. After we'd exited his car, Mazzy had leaned through his passenger window as if she were saying goodbye to a long-lost friend. Tired of waiting, I'd eventually ditched her and headed up to our room.

Guess they hit it off.

"Mazzy. Can I speak to you?" I'd hissed from the bathroom as soon as I saw them tumbling on her bed.

"What? Oh. Sure," she said, pushing herself up and running over to me with a bright smile on her face.

The guy on the bed waved at me. "Hey, sis, why don't you join us? I got enough love in me for the both of you," he said, pointing at his crotch.

Ohforchristssake.

I was surprised he didn't just whip it out for me. Maybe if I'd given him another moment, he would have.

It wasn't like my sister to have such rock-bottom taste. She didn't always bring home the best guys, but this one was a record-breaker.

I pulled Mazzy into the bathroom and closed the

door, leaving the Uber driver fantasizing about having landed a coveted sister-threesome.

"Really, Maz? Are you kidding me?"

Her smiled faltered but only for a second. "He's nice. And I *am* on vacation," she whined.

"We're sharing a fucking room, Maz!"

She sighed and threw up her arms. "Okay, Rain. Okay. I'll kick him out. But thanks. Thanks, *sis*, for your understanding."

Oh no she didn't.

Dammit. I always caved with her.

"Fine," I said, poking my finger in her chest, "you're gonna owe me for this. I'll give you one hour. That's all. Do whatever you have to do and get rid of him."

I grabbed my shoes and purse and split, slamming the bedroom door, the guy calling after me, "Hey! Where you going? Geez, so uptight."

As I headed for the elevators, I also heard the security latch lock from the inside of the room.

Assholes.

If they weren't done in an hour, the shit would hit the fan.

But I wasn't going to share all this with Handsome Elevator Man, even if he had pointed out I was having a less-than-perfect night. Actually, morning.

I sighed as the elevator neared the lobby level, and then—I don't know what came over me—I turned to him. "Hey, I was thinking of getting a drink."

He probably thought I was a loser for getting a wild hair about alcohol at that hour. Whatever.

A weird guy tagged behind him, and cripes was he bad news—looking me up and down like he'd never seen a freaking woman before.

With a loud *ding*, the elevator doors *finally* opened to the lobby, where you would have thought it was the middle of the day with the buzz of activity going on. The slot machines were clanging, bachelorette party-goers were stumbling, and the cleaning crew looked bedraggled and miserable.

I looked up at the cute guy and realized I didn't want him to leave. Why couldn't my sister have brought someone like *him* back to the room? Not that I would have gone for a threesome even with him—that's not my jam—but I would have understood her decision a little better.

Maybe.

"So what are you guys doing in town?" I asked brightly. Anything to keep the cute one around.

He glanced at his companion. Such an odd couple they made—he was so elegant and gorgeous and the other was sad and tacky.

"I live here in Vegas," he said. "I was just… saying hello to some friends."

Saying hi to friends at three a.m.? Okay, Vegas was weirder than I thought.

"What about you?" he asked.

9

Of course that question was eventually going to make its way to me. It was only fair.

"I'm here from LA for the weekend with my sister, attending a birthday party for one of our friends."

I didn't add that it would be the last time I would ever share a room with my sister, or even come to Vegas. Everyone and their mother wanted to party here, where they could cut loose and do shit they'd never consider pulling closer to home.

Like pick up Uber drivers.

The last time I'd been dragged to Vegas, it had been for a friend's divorce party. I'd practically had to sleep in the hallway, that's how busy my roommate was with her new male friend.

Of course, my issue would have been solved, at least partially, by getting my own room. I could easily afford it. Which was part of my problem. I actually could easily afford most anything I wanted, to be honest, thanks to my dad's successful shipping business.

But I didn't want anyone to know that. It was my dirty secret, and I spent a lot of energy hiding it. I was an aspiring artist, and if anyone knew my family was loaded, they'd conclude I was a dilettante, or worse, a hack hobbyist whose parents were buying my way into prestigious galleries and the like.

I couldn't risk it.

It had not taken me long to witness this bias, having overheard my gossipy art school friends talk about another student in our classes.

"That girl, Evan. No talent at all. But she'll do fine, thanks to her family money."

The irony was that Evan was one of the most talented oil painters in our class. Money had nothing to do with her talent. But people make their crappy assumptions, especially in the ultra-competitive world of fine art.

So when I had weekends away with friends, even if my sister joined us, we shared rooms like all the thrifty girls did. No need to show off our shit.

"So, are you having fun so far?" Handsome Guy asked, his weaselly friend one step behind him.

What was that all about?

"Uh, yes. Sure," I forced myself to say.

Yeah, if fun was having your sister do some stranger in your room when you were so tired you wanted to cry. Good times.

He smiled and nodded, and damn if the dimples I'd spotted in the elevator didn't spring to life and scream *look how cute I am*! as if they needed pointing out to begin with.

Seriously, he was tall, so tall that in my bare feet I had to take a step back and look up at him. He had tousled dark hair—messy without trying too hard—which had always been my kryptonite, and heavy brows, an impeccable balance to his perfect lips.

Which, by the way, he had just licked.

Down girl.

He tilted his head. "You don't sound very convincing. I hate to hear of people not having fun in Vegas. If you don't, you might not come back. We need return customers." He laughed again.

Good-looking *and* a sense of humor? Sign me up.

But was he smart? I only did smart.

I swung my shoes and purse nervously, and made my offer again. "Hey, why don't you guys come get a drink with me at the Rotunda bar over here? My treat." I took a step in the bar's direction, thinking they'd follow.

What was the harm in a little company? I didn't particularly like drinking alone, and had to kill some time while my sister boinked her Uber boyfriend.

There would be no more getting kicked out of hotel rooms. I'd reached my lifetime limit. I needed my sleep. And why couldn't she have gone back to the guy's place, anyway?

Wait a minute. That would not have been good. If she'd done that, I'd have had no idea where she'd gone. And I *was* the older sister. I had to keep tabs on the girl. As the family baby, she was not exactly known for practical or responsible decisions.

I bent to put my shoes on and my feet screamed in pain as if they were telling me they were off-duty for the night—*no more heels, Rain. Please?*

But I strapped the bad boys back on so I didn't look like a total hick. Walking around a hotel barefoot was not the classiest—or most sanitary—thing a girl could do.

And thanks to my shoes, my height instantly jumped a good three inches, leaving my new friend and me closer to eye-to-eye level. His unfortunate friend, however, was more shrimpy than ever.

"C'mon," I said, gesturing toward the bar. "Join me. I'm buyin'."

He looked at his companion and shook his head. "We need to head out."

Well crap.

I looked at my watch. "All right, then. It is awfully late, isn't it? You gentlemen have a nice evening. Or should I say a nice morning?" I dropped my head back, laughing, and headed over to the circular bar in the middle of the casino floor.

CHAPTER 2

RAIN

AT THIS 'OFF' hour, if there even were 'off' hours in Vegas, the disheveled people sitting around the bar weren't exactly perky. No, in fact, they just looked plain worn out. But who was I to judge? I wasn't at the top of my game at that moment, either.

I grabbed a seat next to a man who, while he held a beer bottle in his hand, had dozed off, his head hanging down against his chest. I caught the eye of the bartender who nodded as if to say 'yeah, I know.'

Ugh. How sucky would it be to have that job?

"Hi. I'll have a glass of champagne, please."

He seemed happy to be dealing with someone who still had most of their faculties intact.

"Comin' right up. Shall I charge it to your room?" he asked.

I nodded.

The guy next to me snored lightly, so I turned on my stool to face away.

And who did I see making his way over but my elevator friend. And his tag-along buddy.

He grabbed the stool next to me, turning to make sure his friend sat, too.

"You decided you wanted a drink after all," I said, waving the bartender over.

The man nodded, catching my gaze with his piercing light brown eyes.

So piercing.

He nodded, keeping one eye on his friend. "Ya know, it's not every day that a beautiful woman offers to get me a drink."

I blushed. I'd been told I was pretty before, and while I was nothing special, I couldn't remember ever having been paid a compliment by a man like him.

I extended my hand. "I'm Rain."

"Rain? Cool name. I'm Nico. This is my friend here... Dan." He turned to the bartender. "Two Stellas, please."

"And put it on my bill," I called after him.

It felt good to say that. I was tired of acting broke all the time. It stressed me, the constant pretending.

My sister was so paranoid about people discovering our background that she never bought anyone drinks, preferring to order the cheapest wine or beer on a menu so she looked perpetually broke. It worked, especially since we both drove old Toyota Priuses. Which confounded my Mercedes-driving mother.

"So you guys live here in Vegas?" I asked. "Did you grow up here?"

Dan looked at his beer, and Nico shook his head. "I'm from the East Coast. New York, actually. I moved out here not long ago with friends for a... business opportunity."

"Cool," I said, ordering another champagne. "What sort of business opportunity?"

He took a moment to answer. "Um... my friends and I invest in casinos."

"Wow. That sounds interesting. Gaming is a unique business, that's for sure." Thanks to my dad, I'd grown up around a lot of investment talk. I wouldn't have minded testing his acumen but didn't want to completely 'out' myself. Lay low. Divulge little or nothing.

"Yeah, gaming is... unique, for sure." He took a swig of his beer.

And as he did, his suit jacket fell open far enough for me to spot the Burberry tag sewn into the lining.

Holy crap. Burberry. Some of the most expensive suits a man could wear.

Who was I dealing with here? Investing in casinos must be good business.

The guys I usually met, mainly through the art scene, were lucky if they could afford clothes from Goodwill.

"And you?" he asked me. "What do you do?"

"I teach art at a non-profit center for kids, and I study fine art—oil painting, actually—at the LA Academy. I... I'm an artist. I guess."

Why did I always stumble over that? *Imposter syndrome,* I think it was called. That old fear that you're not really any good and never will be.

He frowned, checking on his weird friend again. "What do you mean *you guess?* Sounds to me like you are a bona fide artist."

I shrugged.

"Say it," he said, smiling. "Say *I am an artist.*"

When I hesitated, he said it again, nudging me lightly. "C'mon now. I want to hear you say it."

"You do?" I laughed. "Why?"

He smacked his hand down on the bar. "Because, modesty is bullshit. You're holding yourself back."

Geez.

I'd just met this guy and he already had my number. Cripes, I was in trouble if I were that transparent.

"Okay. Fine. I'm an *artist,*" I mumbled to make him happy.

Why was that so hard to say?

Nico shook his head furiously and held his hand up to his ear. "What? I can't hear you."

I leaned closer to him. "I am an—"

He raised both hands like a *stop* sign.

Was he intentionally embarrassing me?

"Don't say it like it's a secret. I want to hear you call it out," he demanded in a loud voice.

Oh my god.

It was coming up on four a.m. in a Vegas casino, and the only sentient beings were people who were up way past their bedtimes, and it showed. They were dragging their tired asses from one slot machine to the next, or ponying up for one final cocktail before hitting the sack. And then there was the guy sitting next to me, actually sleeping at the bar.

Nobody, and I mean, not a single soul, was paying any attention to me and my new friends. So, why couldn't I have a little fun with Nico's encouragement? Instead, I wanted to crawl away and hide. I would have been more comfortable had I been naked, singing *The Star Spangled Banner*.

Maybe it wasn't what others thought of me that was bothersome. Maybe it was what *I thought of me.*

Christ, who knew that a chance meeting in a hotel elevator would result in a freaking epiphany?

For heaven's sake, I was not only studying art, but I also taught it. I was proud of what I was doing, and fuck anyone who wanted to diminish that.

So I rose from my chair. Champagne held high, I hollered, "I. Am. An—"

And as I did, my heel caught the rung of the stool. After a millisecond of flailing, I realized I was going down. My champagne glass flew out of my right hand when I clutched at the bar for something stationary with my left. Unfortunately, the only thing I came away with was my purse, which, as I went down, also flew out of my grasp. I braced myself for a massive wipeout, watching my spilled champagne turn into a foamy puddle that was eagerly slurped up by the casino carpeting.

Floor, meet Rain.

I went down in a crumpled pile. Was this the universe's way of keeping me in check? Or making sure I didn't get too high and mighty?

Good work, universe. Thanks a million.

Nico had reached for me but I went over too fast for him to help. A couple people actually turned my way but, unimpressed, turned right back to whatever they'd been doing.

Then, as I began to push myself up, Nico's friend Dan popped out of his seat.

Thank goodness. He might have looked kind of dirtbaggy, but he deserved props for his gentlemanly rush to my aid. I smiled at him and reached for his help.

But as he got closer, he didn't take my hand. In fact, he didn't even look at me.

Instead, his gaze was fixed on my purse.

The bastard stepped over me, grabbed it, and started to run.

CHAPTER 3

RAIN

I TURNED to watch Dan take off, my handbag under his arm like a football, with Nico sprinting after him in close pursuit.

As if getting kicked out of my room by my sister wasn't bad enough, I'd now been robbed by the two fuckers I'd just bought drinks for. They'd probably set the whole thing up.

I was pissed.

And being *pissed* gives you energy.

I kicked off the heels that had been the source of my clumsiness and jumped to my feet. The purse thieves were heading toward some sort of service door.

Not tonight, bitch.

I hit the ground running. There was no other way to put it. Two major insults in one night was just going too far. I wasn't going to take being robbed sitting down. Or lying down.

Those assholes hadn't counted on my being a former track star. Sure, it had been a long time since I'd run a sprint—like *high school* long time ago—but I was going to give it my best shot.

They disappeared through a door that said *employees only*. I glanced around and saw no one paying any attention, other than a tired-looking man sweeping in a corner. When I hesitated at the door, he gave me the slightest nod as if to say *go for it*.

What the hell.

I yanked the door open to see Dan and Nico bolting down a long hallway lined with closed doors. I took off after them. Not far ahead of me, Dan swerved into a stairwell, and from the sound of their shoes pounding on the stairs, they were headed into the bowels of the hotel's underground.

I picked up speed when I lost sight of them, the pounding of my bare feet on the cold floor jolting my ankles and making a *slap, slap, slap* sound. I wasn't sure which was more miserable—wearing torturous heels or running barefoot—but I was so pissed the discomfort barely registered.

Following the *clump, clump, clump* of the guys down the echo-y stairs, I amazed myself that I was actually keeping up with them, if not gaining ground. One flight down, another door swung open so hard it smashed into the stairwell's cinderblock walls, announcing the exact direction they'd headed in.

Fuckers. They thought they could rip me off? Well, they had another think coming.

My purse didn't have much in it besides a wallet I'd picked up at Ann Taylor, and a couple twenty-dollar bills. Oh, and my favorite Chanel lipstick—I couldn't completely deny myself, could I?—but it was the principle, dammit.

No one was stealing my shit.

Just as I burst through the stairwell door—the one the guys had nearly ripped off its hinges—a deafening explosion left my ears ringing and my heart pounding. I froze, pressing myself against the cold basement wall.

What *was* that?

Had I gotten in over my head?

Dumb question. Of course I had. I was somewhere in the basement of the Venetian Hotel, and there was not a soul around as far as I could see—except for my purse thieves. All that lay ahead of me was a darkened hallway.

Maybe it was time for my pursuit to end. I didn't need to be some sort of hero over an inexpensive bag and wallet holding, at most, fifty bucks.

The lipstick could be replaced with one trip to the mall.

But I was a curious bugger, and couldn't help but inch forward—silently, thanks to my bare feet—to see what the hell had happened and where the guys had gone.

I hugged the wall, painted a sad basement yellow, chipped and scarred most likely by clumsy carts transporting towels and other hotel things.

Since I'd stopped running and the blood had ceased roaring in my ears, the surrounding quiet created a stark contrast to the casino floor above, where slot machine bells rang non-stop and the general Vegas din never ceased.

That's when it dawned on me just how far I was from help, should I need it, and how close I was to danger, given that I was in a deserted basement *and* in close proximity to criminals.

Shit.

I knew I should turn around and go. Just tiptoe right out of there. Purse snatching was a petty crime as crimes went, but if the thieves were opportunists, god knew what else they'd do if they got their hands on me with no one around to help.

Did that stop me creeping down the hall toward the racket I'd heard?

Hell no.

I stole toward the dark until I was immersed in it, and the further I got, the stronger a strange burning smell became.

My eyes adjusting to the dark, I fingered the frame of a closed door. Quiet sounds came from behind it.

"Help me. Help me," a man whimpered.

I pressed my ear against it.

"Sorry, fucker. You don't deserve help."

Was that Nico? And if so, was Dan begging for help? How's that? I thought they were in cahoots.

"You never should have stolen that woman's bag. You might have actually lived a little longer. But you just signed your own death warrant."

Holy shit. That *was* Nico speaking.

"No man, don't do it—"

A second explosion jolted me back to reality. This time it had been close enough to leave my ears ringing until I was dizzy. And that smell. That burning smell.

That was a goddamn gun.

I broke into a sprint back toward the stairs I'd come down, but in my panic, I couldn't find the right door— they all looked alike and each handle I turned was locked.

Fuck.

I could see it now.

Woman who was found dead in basement of Venetian Hotel was an art student and daughter of the very rich—

Oh, and I could hear my sister's comments.

Um, well, she was in the room and left to go down and get a drink in the lobby. I never saw her again.

She'd sob for the TV cameras. She was good with the waterworks. 'Course she'd never mention her booty call. She'd throw me under the bus even in death.

I frantically turned one doorknob after the other, when the door where the gunshot had come from swung open with a creak. I whipped around a corner to hide.

Had I been fast enough?

I tiptoed down the hall toward another bend in the corridor, trying to get as far away from the approaching footsteps as possible, when a quiet voice called after me.

"Hey. Where are you going?"

I whipped around to see Nico holding my handbag, confusion covering his face.

"Oh. Hi," I said in a trembling voice, as if he were the last person in the world I expected to see.

God, I was an idiot.

He moved toward me, and I took a step back, my hands held up in surrender.

"Please don't hurt me. I won't report this to anyone. I'll stay quiet."

He smiled, amused. "I know you won't tell anyone. Here's your purse, by the way. I got it back for you."

I let him approach me and handing the bag over, he took my hand—odd behavior for a thief and murderer, but who was I to argue? He led me to a nearby freight elevator and pressed the *up* button.

Time to get the hell out of there. Alone.

"Thanks, Nico. I really appreciate it. I'm pretty tired now, so I'm just gonna go back up to my room. It was nice meeting you." I smiled and put my purse over my shoulder, heading for the staircase I'd come down not ten minutes earlier. I was trying to act completely normal, like I wasn't trying to get away from a guy with a gun in the basement of a giant hotel while barefoot.

He grabbed my hand more tightly, as if he'd not heard my polite goodbye. "This will take us to the loading dock. From there, we'll head out."

He yanked my hand when he realized I was glued to the floor.

"C'mon," he said, with another tug.

"Um, no thanks, Nico. I think I'll go. My sister will be looking for me."

Shaking his head, he furrowed his brow. "Rain, that's not possible. You're coming with me."

The jaw-like doors of the freight elevator opened, and he pulled me into the cavernous space, pressing a button to close the doors and then another button that said *LD*.

Loading dock?

"I... I don't have any shoes," I stumbled.

"You don't do you?" he asked with a chuckle. "Seems like you're always barefoot."

He guided me out of the freight elevator as soon as the doors opened and through another, smaller door that opened into the hotel lobby.

CHAPTER 4

RAIN

How'd he know his way around so well?

The noise and bright lights we burst into made me want to shrink, but there was no slowing with as fast as Nico was walking, his long legs covering twice as much as mine per step.

He leaned close to me, and I realized how good he smelled. "We'll get you some shoes."

Gee, thanks.

We walked out in front of the hotel where the valets were running back and forth parking cars. Over to the side was a line of yellow taxis. Given the hour, few people were waiting.

That never happened in Vegas. You always had to wait.

Nico, still holding my hand, started toward them.

"Wait. Wait just a minute," I hissed, not wanting to attract attention.

He whipped around. "What? We need to get out of here."

"But my sister—"

I tried to yank my hand out of his, but his grip was too tight.

"*Wait*. First of all, did you kill that man back there—?"

But before I could finish my question, his lips sealed over mine. With his hand behind my neck, I was pinned to him.

Yup. I was kissing a purse thief and murderer right there in front of The Venetian, where I'd exited an Uber only an hour before.

He moved his mouth next to my ear. "Put your arms arout me, Rain. Kiss me back."

Was he fucking kidding?

"No!" I said, pushing him away.

He pulled me closer, and jerking his chin toward two cop cars just pulling up. "See? Now kiss me. They'll completely overlook us."

Why did we need to be overlooked?

Oh right, that murder thing. I'd done nothing wrong, though. Why the hell did I need to hide?

But because he was holding me so tightly, I turned my mouth to his, strictly for practical purposes, as I heard the cops get out of their cars and start looking around.

There were worse ways to throw somebody off than making out with a gorgeous man.

Nico's lips were firm but not aggressive, parting only slightly as though he didn't want to push me too far. He held me by weaving his hands through my hair and holding fistfuls of it. Under another circumstance, I would have been thrilled.

A small moan vibrated his lips against mine, and an electric jolt shot right down into my expensive Carine Gillmore panties, reminding me how long it had been since I'd been kissed.

Yes, I wore expensive undies. My classmates weren't privy to them, so I figured, *why not?* It was one of my few indulgences since undertaking the identity of a starving teacher/student/artist.

I instinctively parted my lips just enough to invite Nico's probing tongue, which tasted me with a confidence I didn't think I'd ever experienced with a man—criminal or otherwise.

No big surprise, really. A gorgeous man like he probably got nookie all day, every day. He was an *expert* in matters relating to the female body, no doubt about it.

Wait. What the fuck was I doing, normalizing making out with a *criminal*? I should have been disgusted by the vile man.

I tried to pull away. "Nico, um, this is not—"

He pressed his lips to mine once more, slowly

turning me with one open eye so he could see where the cops had gone.

Then, he released me so abruptly I almost fell backward.

"Jesus. Thanks," I said, straightening my hair and dress, and glancing toward the door the cops had just disappeared through. Could I make a quick getaway?

Don't forget, he has a gun, dumbass.

"Let's grab this cab," he said, heading toward the closest one's open door.

Yeah right. I wasn't going anywhere. I didn't care how well he kissed.

"No. My sister is upstairs. And besides, I have questions."

He looked around and walked me to the bench usually reserved for people waiting for a cab.

He spoke just next to my ear. "What do you need to know? Aside from the fact that we need to get out of here?"

I held my hands up like a *stop* sign. "First, did you kill that man? With your gun? You know, did you shoot him? Until he was dead?"

He looked at me like I had two heads. "Yeah. Of course I did. He was a... well, he stole your purse."

Another cop car pulled up, lights flashing. The officers left their car in the middle of the drive and ran inside, their hands on their weapons.

Jesus.

"Isn't that kind of an extreme punishment? And

wasn't he your friend?" I hissed. "Who the hell shoots his friend for stealing a purse?"

Now he looked at me like I had *four* heads. "He wasn't my friend. What made you think that?"

Was he serious?

"Why was he hanging out with you?" I asked. "Why was he having a beer with us while we talked about whether or not I was a real artist? You know, shooting the shit, like friends do."

He nodded. "Right. Okay. I'll explain everything. Please just get in the cab with me."

He started walking, and since he was holding my hand, I had little choice but to follow.

What the fuck? I was getting in a cab with a stranger who killed people. I slipped my hand to the door handle, hoping he didn't notice. How much would it hurt to jump out in speeding traffic?

Once inside, Nico passed the driver a couple twenties. "Can you take us to The Mirage, please?"

The cabbie hit the breaks and looked over his shoulder, holding the money between his fingers. "Sir, The Mirage is right across the street. Are you sure you want me to drive you there? It would be quicker to walk."

"Yes, I'm sure," Nico said in a tone that was about as final as final could be.

The night—or should I say morning—was getting weirder by the moment. I'd just gotten into a cab with a stranger, who, by the way, was also a murderer. It was looking like I was no smarter than my sister.

"I need to call Mazzy." I pulled my phone out of my purse.

But as soon as I did, Nico snatched it away. "I'll keep that for now." He dropped it into his jacket pocket. "And who is Mazzy?"

"My sister. Now, give me that," I hissed, trying not to attract the cabbie's attention.

But he ignored me, and as we pulled into the drive at The Mirage, he leaned next to my ear. "Stay close to me."

I supposed I was in no position to argue. There were no cops in sight. I could run to the valet or bellman but what good would that do? Nico had a weapon, and they most likely did not.

We popped out of the cab as the driver took off, shaking his head at the craziness of making forty bucks for driving two blocks.

Nico took my hand again, and we crossed the asphalt to a valet stand where a couple pimply teenage boys laughed and nudged each other. They straightened up when they saw us approaching.

Yeah, they would have been real heroes had I gone to them for assistance.

"May we help you, sir?" one of them asked.

"Yup. That's my BMW over there. You got the key for me?" he asked, handing over a twenty.

"Um, do you have your ticket, sir?"

Nico stared the kid down. "I already gave it to you. Remember?"

I looked at Nico, who continued to glare at the valet, who just looked confused until his friend stepped up.

"Yes, sir, I remember you. The keys are in the ignition."

Nico nodded at them both. "Thank you, gentlemen. Have a good day."

I was pretty sure the BMW *wasn't* Nico's car.

But he held the passenger door open for me like a regular gentleman, hopped in the driver side, and drove away as I buckled my seatbelt.

It was the most normal thing I'd do for the next several days.

CHAPTER 5

NICO

"I'm pretty sure you just stole a car," Rain said from the passenger seat, turning over her shoeless feet to look at their disgusting black soles.

I steered into traffic and grabbed the first freeway onramp I came across. If the BMW was some tourist's car, they'd be looking for it on the Strip. At least initially.

Geez, those valet chumps caved without any trouble. Their heads would roll later, but that wasn't my problem.

No, my problem was the lovely woman sitting next to me, whose feet were bare and getting filthier by the minute.

"Rain, I'm not sure I would call it *stealing*, per se," I said. "More like borrowing. The owners will get it back. If I'm in a good mood, I might even refill the gas tank."

Rain slapped her forehead with an *ah-ha* movement. "Right. Great idea. Next you're gonna say you'll pay for the funeral arrangements for the man you just killed."

Well. The pretty lady was funny. I liked that.

"He was not a nice man. He got what he deserved."

I said no more. My business was strictly on a need-to-know basis, and while this woman was a witness, the less she knew, the better it would be for everyone.

Not that she could deal with the truth, anyway. Few people could. There was some ugly shit in this world that people like me knew to keep to ourselves.

She *harrumphed* loudly. "He stole my purse. That's all. I don't like having my purse stolen, but I wouldn't say that deserves a death sentence."

She had a lot to learn.

"He did much more than that—"

"Are you goddamn crazy? You're a murderer and car thief, and not to mention, now a kidnapper. And you forced me to kiss you. That's assault, if I'm not mistaken. I'm not down with this joy ride, and I'm definitely not down with your hanging on to my phone. Please just take me back to my hotel. My sister will be wondering where I am. I'll forgive and forget. I'm feeling generous, today. You are lucky."

She was the lucky one. She just didn't know it yet.

I shook my head. "Sorry. Can't do that."

"What?" she screamed. "This is bullshit!"

Convinced I'd thrown off anyone who might have been following us, I headed back to the Bellagio to the giant parking garage behind it, where I'd left my own car. I'd ditch the 'borrowed' vehicle, and w'd be good to go. Couldn't be too careful in my line of work.

I had some questions of my own for Rain. "Let me ask you this. What possessed you to run after us? In your bare feet?"

We returned to the surface streets, and as the day was getting lighter, I noticed her fingers grasping the door handle as we approached a red light. I reached across the front seat's console, and with my right hand, grasped her left wrist. Tightly. She wasn't going anywhere.

"Really?" she said, looking at my hand on her arm. God, she was fucking beautiful with those bright eyes lit by the morning sun, and even sexier with them full of anger.

My kryptonite. A feisty woman.

"Do you have to hold me with that death grip? It's not exactly comfortable, you know."

Her comfort at that point was not a priority. Her safety, however, was. She had no idea how stupid it had been to follow me and the fucker I'd had to kill. And now that she'd witnessed his murder, she was directly in harm's way. My colleagues Luca and Leo were not going to be happy I'd picked up an unexpected friend, but I couldn't very well have left her in the basement of the Venetian. I wasn't sure who would have arrived on the scene first—the team that the dead fucker had been part of, or the cops, some of whom were *paid* by the team the dead fucker had been part of.

Either way, she would have been screwed had she been found, most likely ending up just like the guy I'd put the bullet in.

"Nico. You did say your name was Nico, right?"

I nodded. "Yes, I did say that."

"Nico. I can give you money. If you just let me off here... or anywhere, really, I can make sure you get a large sum of cash. And, I promise, I won't tell a soul I ever laid eyes on you or your friend." Her voice was growing shriller by the moment.

"And furthermore—"

I was done with her attempts at negotiation.

"Shut up. Rain, please shut up," I said, speaking over her. I didn't like being a dick, but she needed to understand the gravity of the situation she was in.

Her mouth dropped open as we pulled into the garage where I'd left my SUV. I was getting a clearer picture of who I was dealing with. I supposed she was, too.

The woman was used to getting her way.

"The man I killed—his name was not Dan. I'm not even sure of his real name. But he was not my friend."

I pulled the borrowed BMW into a parking spot out of view of the garage's security cameras.

I knew where the security cameras were in nearly

every garage in town. It was part of being good at what I did.

Releasing her wrist, I spoke in a calm tone. "That guy was a very bad man. He did a lot more than steal purses." I hesitated before I dropped my bomb.

"He trafficked women."

There. I'd done it.

She frowned, and her mouth dropped open. "Um. What?"

It wasn't an easy thing to hear.

"He captures women, takes them out of the country, and rents or even sells them. That's what a trafficker is, and that's what that guy did. He became known to my business partners and me and we decided to do something about him."

The color in her pretty face drained, and she looked like she might get sick. "Uh... um, why not just call the police?" she asked.

It was a good question, the first one I would have asked, too, if I'd not already known more about the gruesome underbelly of human trafficking.

"The police do not have the... resources we do. It takes them much longer to make an arrest, and most of the time, the perp gets out right away because the trafficking organizations have a ton of money. The normal channels aren't moving fast enough. They aren't able to."

She took a deep breath and leaned back on the headrest. "I don't feel so well," she said.

I placed my hand on the back of her neck. "Yeah. It's pretty sickening." I opened the car windows for some air.

I'd have been lying if I didn't admit that touching Rain, however innocently, got my motor revving. Of course I barely knew her, but there was something... I couldn't put my finger on. And to think I'd come across her in an elevator, and that *she'd* been the one to insist I join her for a drink. And then there had been that fake kiss we'd shared... which had seemed so fucking real.

Bizarro.

"You gonna be okay?" I asked.

She nodded slowly.

"Okay then. Let's ditch this car and get into mine."

I threw the ignition keys on the BMW's floor and hustled around to the passenger side, taking Rain by the hand. She followed weakly, and a few spaces down, I helped her into my car. Once I was in the driver's side, I pressed the door locks.

Old habit.

"If you weren't helping him steal my purse, Nico, why'd you go after him?" she asked like she didn't really want to know.

I took a deep breath. "Because, Rain, if he'd gotten your personal information, you could very well have ended up on his list."

She gasped. "Oh god," she moaned. "Oh god."

I would have done anything to protect her from the ugly side of Vegas, but we were well beyond that point.

"There's a ring, a team of these guys trolling around town, looking for beautiful women. They work to get in your good graces, and when your guard is down, they find a way to get up to your room. He might have nabbed you and your friend."

"Sister," she corrected.

"Right. Sister. The really fucked up thing is that they are often car share drivers. You know, Uber, Lyft, etcetera. Those services are so popular now that it's easy pickings."

She emitted a strangled cry and flung the car door open just in time to be sick on the parking garage floor.

Damn. She took the news hard. Harder than I'd expected.

"Here's some water," I said, grabbing a half-full bottle from my car's console.

She shook her head hard, as if to clear cobwebs, and took a small sip, waving her free hand like a maniac.

She was gasping now, like she might hyperventilate.

"Nico," she said in a small voice, holding her stomach.

"What's wrong? Are you okay?"

She shook her head, *no*.

Her voice faded to a whisper. "Nico, my sister is up in our hotel room."

"Right. You told me that."

She put her hand over her mouth as a sob exploded.

"Nico, she's up there with an Uber driver. That's

43

why I had to vacate for a while. That's why you saw me in the elevator, pissed off."

Holy fuck.

My heart started to pound, and my thoughts jumped into overdrive. I had to act, and I had to act fast.

I put my hands on either side of her face, and forced her to look at me. "Tell me. Did the guy try to convince you to stay? To hang out with them?"

She nodded, tears streaming down her face. "Y... yes. Do you think they have my sister? Oh god no... please say no..."

CHAPTER 6

RAIN

AN UNGODLY SCREAM erupted from my chest, and I pounded the car's dashboard.

"Take me... back to the Venetian. I have to get to Mazzy. Hurry."

Oh god. My worst nightmare. My little sister...

I slammed my hand on the dash again when Nico didn't move fast enough. I didn't give a shit who he was or that he had a gun. "Goddammit, take me there, NOW!" I screamed between sobs.

Maybe if we got there in time...

Nico reached in his pocket and pulled out his phone. "I have people who can get there faster. What's the room number?"

Fuck. In my panic, I couldn't recall which room

we'd been in. You got off the elevator, and turned left, and then right...

Think, Rain, think.

"Room twelve-fourteen. That's it," I cried.

Nico put his phone up to his ear. "It's me. Yeah. All good. He's taken care of. Hey, help me out. I think there might be some activity in room twelve-fourteen. Can you get up there and check it out? Cool. Make it quick."

He swiped his phone closed.

"Do... do you think they got my sister?"

He put a hand on my shoulder. "I'm sure everything will be fine. It's probably just a coincidence that she picked up an Uber driver. There are thousands of them in Vegas. A coincidence is all it is."

"Well, then. Let's go," I said, pulling on my seat belt.

If we hurried, I figured we could get there just as his contact did.

I thought back to the guy who'd weaseled his way into Mazzy's pants. He was kind of small and skinny. Maybe she could take him. She was no wimp. And we had pepper spray! Oh, wait, *I* was the one with pepper spray. And it was in my purse. The one sitting in my lap right there in Nico's car.

I wracked my brain trying to remember if there were any sharp objects in the nightstand that could serve as a weapon. Maybe she could lead him into the bathroom and beat him with my heavy hair dryer. She could wrap the cord around his neck a couple times and take him out that way—

"We're not going anywhere, Rain. The person I just called will take care of things. We need to sit tight."

Was he kidding?

I shook my head furiously. "The hell we will. This is my sister we're talking about."

He didn't move.

"Fine, I'll go alone."

I started opening the car door when, again, he grabbed my wrist. But this time I yanked myself free. I got out of the car and started running through the parking garage.

He didn't come after me.

But he did roll down his window. "Rain, there is nothing you can do now, and if you go over there and someone has taken your sister, the same will happen to you."

I stopped running.

He continued to call after me. "You'll be faced with some seriously bad people."

Bad people? Did I need to point out that he wasn't exactly *Mother Theresa*?

I turned around, hands on hips. "We can't just sit here and do nothing. That's fucked up. My sister's life is in danger."

He gestured with his head. "Get back in the car."

I couldn't accept that my sister's life might be at stake and I was doing nothing more than sitting in a parking garage with... what *was* this guy's story, anyway?

Against my better judgment, I climbed into the SUV and held out my hand. "Please give me my phone."

He nodded, thick hair falling over his forehead, which he pushed back with his fingers. Casual, but confident. He reached into his pocket and handed me my phone.

Shit, why was I thinking about how hot this criminal was, when I should have been focused on my sister?

Mazzy's phone rang and rang then went straight to voicemail.

I looked at Nico hopefully. "She could be asleep. You know, maybe the guy she picked up went home and she conked out."

He tilted his head, looking at me like I was an idiot.

If the guy she picked up had left, and she decided to get some sleep, wouldn't she have called first to see where I was?

Probably.

But maybe she just fell asleep.

Probably not.

The tears started to come again, and I zeroed in on Nico. "*Who* are you? How do you know this stuff? And why do you kill people and steal cars? And kidnap women? Are you in a gang or something?"

He looked amused, which really pissed me off. "You could sort of say that."

"What the hell does that mean?" I asked through tears.

"Well, my associates and I own a variety of businesses, and like I said… we invest in casinos. That's all you really need to know."

I rolled my eyes at his answer. "Lots of people own businesses, and they don't shoot people. Are you in the mafia or something?"

He just looked at me.

"Well?"

"We… don't really call it that."

Oh for Christ's sake.

"We look at it as more of a family."

Okay, right. Mafia it was. Or some sort of generic organized crime, at the very least. Now I was getting the picture. And it wasn't a pretty one.

His phone rang, and I jumped. I squeezed my eyes shut and pictured my sister, a pretty wisp of a thing who wouldn't hurt a fly.

"Yeah?" he said into the phone. "Really? Shit. Okay."

He turned to me. "When my contact got to the room, your things were there but your sister wasn't. And… there were signs of a struggle."

Another sob escaped my lips. My sister. My younger sister. She was irresponsible and flighty, but I adored her.

Would I ever see her again?

Oh god.

I doubled over in my seat and pounded my thighs with my fists. How could this happen?

"It's my fault," I sobbed. "I should have stood my

ground and insisted the guy leave. Mazzy, oh Mazzy," I moaned.

Nico rubbed the back of my head, his fingers tangling through my hair.

"Rain, it wouldn't have mattered. Once they have a mark, they move on it. In fact, you were lucky you left the room. And, believe it or not, even luckier you ran into me."

Wiping the tears that wouldn't stop, I looked up at him. "I'm lucky I met you? Nothing personal, but I'm not so sure about that."

Maybe another time, another place, when I wasn't hysterical about my sister and I could just focus on how damn hot he was, I might have felt lucky.

But not then.

"Think about it, Rain. If our paths hadn't crossed, you'd have no idea what happened to Mazzy. I wouldn't be around to help you find her, and chances are you'd end up in the same boat."

He started his car's engine. Where the hell were we going now?

"What do you mean? Can you really help me find my sister?" I asked, my heart in my throat.

He gave me a serious look. "I can help you, yes. That doesn't mean we'll find her, but with my... resources, we have a good shot at it."

I took a deep breath. "Nico?"

"Yeah?" He steered us out of the parking garage and onto the street.

I knew I shouldn't ask what I was about to, but I had to. Mazzy was my sister, and if she was going to suffer, I was, too.

"What... what do they do to women, these traffickers?" I asked in a small voice.

He stole a glance at me, clearly considering whether or not he should answer, and whether or not I truly wanted him to.

He took a deep breath. "They sell the women. Like cattle at an auction. Or they imprison them in brothels. They are usually taken out of the country very quickly and, unfortunately, are never heard from again."

CHAPTER 7

RAIN

A LONG, loud cry scared the crap out of me.

And then I realized it had been me.

I couldn't breathe. I couldn't see. And all I could feel were my fists pounding on the car around me.

The pain was exquisite and unrelenting. A thousand knives stabbing at me in the knowledge that my little sister was going to suffer. I had to take it away from her. Shoulder the burden.

Universe, let it be me. Let me trade places with her.

I'd do anything. Anything to spare her.

Nico turned a corner and slammed on the breaks, pinning my arms in a bear hug.

"I'm sorry, Rain. I'm sorry. I shouldn't have told you the truth. Sometimes I can't even face it. That's why my partners and I have taken a stand. We're going to stop this, so help me."

"Mazzy, Mazzy, Mazzy," I kept mumbling.

I don't know how long I was weeping into Nico's chest, but when my breath steadied, I pulled back from him just enough to see my day-old makeup smudged all over his starched white dress shirt.

I must have been disgusting with tears and snot all over my face, but I looked up at him anyway.

"Why? Why do you care so much about this, Nico?"

"The guys who do this, they used to... work with us. Standard organized syndicate stuff. But they got into trafficking and never looked back. It's lucrative. Very lucrative. Just shows how many sick fucks there are in the world, willing to buy and sell other human beings for their own profit and pleasure."

"And the police? They don't do anything?" I asked.

He tilted his head. "They try. But like I said, they have limited resources and can't move as quickly as we do. Plus," he said, looking directly at me, "they have to follow the law. We don't."

"What do you mean, you don't have to follow the law?"

Shrugging, he said, "We have a different way of doing things, my associates and I."

He wasn't kidding. Like killing, stealing, and kidnapping.

"I see. Then, what's next?" I asked. "What do we do about my sister now that she's been abducted?"

The very words made me want to kill someone.

He took my hands. "We wait. I know that's not what you want to hear, but I have people watching the ring carrying out this shit, and we'll know something soon."

I looked out the window at an empty, dusty lot. "You can take me back to the hotel, then. I'll pick up the stuff in our room, get my car, and head back to LA. I guess I need to tell my parents what's going on."

Shit. What *would* I tell my parents? That their darling youngest daughter picked up a man who turned out to be the worst kind of criminal?

Nico cleared his throat. "Unfortunately, Rain, that's not an option."

"Huh? *What's* not an option?" I asked.

"None of those things are options—not going back to your room, not getting your car, not going home."

I laughed. I was so not in the mood for bullshit.

"Whatever. Take me to the hotel."

He pulled the car back into traffic as I composed myself.

"For one thing, Rain, you aren't safe. I think I've already told you that. For another, you've witnessed some things you shouldn't have. I need to take you with me."

What the—? He claimed he wasn't a trafficker, and yet he was forcing me to go somewhere with him? What kind of bullshit was that?

I shook my head, trying to think clearly to find a way out of the situation.

"Look, Nico. I won't tell a soul what I saw, and I won't even tell anyone we think my sister's been trafficked. I'll make something up and let you guys do your thing. I won't even notify the police as long as you're working on my sister's situation."

That sounded reasonable, right? More than reasonable, actually. If he'd just drop me at the hotel, I could gather my sister's crap and be on the road to LA in less than an hour.

Preferably with shoes on.

But I realized we were not going to the hotel when Nico headed for the freeway.

"You *are* a trafficker!" I cried.

He'd tricked me. He wasn't going to do anything to find Mazzy, and was throwing me right in the pit with her.

I had to think of something. The further we got from The Venetian, the less likely it was that I'd ever get back there and the less likely it was that I'd ever be a free woman again. I looked around the car for something, anything, that I could use as a weapon.

I had my phone. I could call the police. But if what Nico had said was true…

I came up empty. Unless I could get my hands on his gun.

"I'm not a trafficker, I told you. Look, I'll make a deal with you. You come home with me and I'll keep looking for Mazzy. If you leave, the deal's off. I can't protect you, and I won't be looking for your sister."

My head spun in his direction. "What? You're extorting me? You fucker!" I screamed. "And how do I know you'll look for my sister, anyway?"

The tears threatened again, but this time I vowed to control them. I couldn't be a help to Mazzy if I couldn't help myself first.

Remain calm...

After fifteen minutes of silence and wracking my brains over the few, unappealing options I had, we pulled up to what looked like a big resort with a locked gate over the drive. Nico pressed a button, and a towering iron fence creaked open.

"What is this?" I asked. "The place where you take kidnapped women?"

The saving grace was that if it were, I might see my sister.

Multiple buildings dotted the property—huge houses, little cottages, and other outbuildings I couldn't identify. It was perfectly manicured in a desert-y landscape sort of way, with cactus, succulents, and palm trees. And there was a badass-looking motorcycle parked outside a multiple-car garage.

"This is where I live with my business partners, Dom and Colt. I think of it as a bit of a compound. Or an estate." He pressed the unlock button on the car doors.

"A compound?" I watched a security guard patrol the property with a large firearm in his holster.

Nico got out of the SUV and beckoned me to

follow. I gingerly stepped on the crushed rock covering on the ground, and limped over to him, shading my eyes from the burning sun.

"Hey guys," he called, waving at a couple figures approaching us.

"Hello," they said when they got closer.

In spite of all the shit that had gone down, I was suddenly self-conscious about my disastrous appearance.

"Guys, this is Rain, the sister of the woman we think was grabbed by the traffickers," Nico said.

"I'm Dom."

"And I'm Colt."

They both smiled and extended their hands.

"Um… uh… hi," I managed to spit out.

Oh. My. God.

When did mobsters—or whatever the hell these guys were—get so good-looking? Seriously. I wanted to crawl away in shame, looking as bedraggled and dirty as I was. I looked down at my filthy feet and now-chipped pedicure, and back up at them, smiling.

"Sorry I'm such a sight. I've been through a rough… well, things have been crazy in the last few hours."

Yeah, like the way I looked was a priority. What an idiot I was.

The one named Dom, in low-hanging jeans and a faded concert T-shirt, put his hands on his hips. "Well, come on in. You can get cleaned up, and we'll get you something to eat." He looked over at Nico.

"We gotta get her some clothes, too. I'll make a call," Colt added, rubbing a hand first through his beard and then over his bald head.

They had access to clothes? *Women's* clothes?

Maybe the weird-ass compound I'd been forced to come to, with its gorgeous men and beautiful houses, wasn't going to be so horrible after all.

CHAPTER 8

NICO

Rain might have actually cheered up a little when she got a load of our nice property, and found that Dom and Colt weren't hard on the eyes, either.

Amazing what some nice scenery could do for a mood.

And in spite of her being a little worse for the wear, the guys appeared to be pleased with her, too.

But that only lasted for a moment. I wasn't surprised.

It was to be expected.

"Why don't you take her over to the Agave cottage?" Colt suggested. "That one's the nicest."

If memory served, my own bedroom had a slightly obstructed view right into the lovely little Agave cottage. How convenient.

Wonder if any of the other guys could see into the Agave windows.

Down boy.

"A cottage," Rain said, "that sounds nice. But, um, what about my sister?"

Colt patted her on the back. "We've got some leads already. I can't say much, but I'm feeling pretty good about locating her."

Locating her was different than *finding* her. But I didn't press it.

I nodded. "If anyone can track your sister down, it's Colt. He knows everyone and everything."

Dom laughed, stuffing his hands in his pockets. "What? Colt doesn't know shit. Nico, you're just sucking up to him to get him working for a change."

I liked our little brotherly bust-up banter. Good for camaraderie. Made it easier to do some of the things we had to do.

I held my hands up. "All right, *ladies.* Let's not get into a catfight. Rain, let's get you to your cottage so you can clean up and rest. I'll have the housekeeper bring you something to eat."

She took a couple steps toward my house, but that was not where she would be staying. Nor would she even step foot inside the place. At least not initially. Seemed like Rain was still getting a grasp on the situation she was in. I didn't blame her. It was a lot to absorb.

"Oh, I can just come with you. I don't really need

anything brought to me." She smiled politely, clearly eager to make a good impression.

Her glances at my house, and those at Dom's and Colt's, made it clear she was curious as hell.

I took a deep breath. "Um, Rain, you can't do that. You have to go to your cottage."

She continued smiling. That dazzling smile, which, even though she was a mess, knocked me sideways. "Thank you, Nico. Your hospitality," she looked around at all three of us, "is amazing. But before we go, do you think I could see your house? Just a quick peek. I *love* that style of Spanish-influenced architecture."

I shook my head. She wasn't getting it. "Sorry, but no. You can't, Rain."

She shrugged. "Well, I can't blame you. I wouldn't want these filthy feet on my floors either."

"Rain, we need to level with you. Even if your feet were clean you still couldn't go in the house,"

"Why? Do you have a wife or something?" Her head fell back with a light laugh.

"No... there are no wives. You can't go because you are relegated to the cottage. You don't have house privileges."

She wrinkled her nose.

"Don't worry. You'll be very comfortable and all your needs will be met."

"But... what do house privileges mean?" She looked at the other guys.

"You are confined to your cottage. You will not be permitted to leave it."

Her mouth dropped open, a sound sort of like *ha* slipping out. She was momentarily speechless.

But not for long.

She hiked her handbag up on her shoulder—the very handbag that had started the whole mess—and planted her hands on her hips.

I kept my thoughts to myself, but she did look pretty damn funny in her *going out with the girls dress* that was now a wrinkled mess, tangled hair with a loose barrette falling out, and of course, bare feet. She was trying to be tough. It wasn't working.

"Um, what? Are you saying I'm a prisoner here? What is up with that?"

Colt stepped in. "I wouldn't go as far as to say that, but for the time being, we need to keep you safe. We need to keep an eye on you."

"That's bullshit!" she yelled, backing away. "I have to get back to teach my classes."

"Call them. Make something up," I said.

She wasn't going anywhere. The place was tight as a fortress. I'd seen she was a fast runner, but once she hit the periphery of our property, unless she could fly, she was stuck within our walls.

I put my hands up like a stop sign. "Rain, you agreed to a deal. Remember?"

Her face was red with fury. "I... I... I agreed to stick around while you looked for my sister. That did

NOT mean I was going to be imprisoned in a cottage."

She pressed her lips together, her temper getting the better of her. "Fuck you. Fuck you all." Her hands flew to her face, which crumbled, and she released a long wail.

"You can shove your *deal* up your asses," she screamed.

Shit. I felt for her, I really did.

I walked over and put an arm around her. "C'mon, Rain. Let's go." I steered her toward the Agave cottage, and though she shook my arm off her shoulders, she walked with me.

I flicked the light on when we arrived, and she scanned her new digs. Regardless of the circumstances, she couldn't complain about her accommodations. The little place was perfect for one person—calling it a cottage didn't really do it justice, with its sweeping living room, state of the art kitchen, bathroom with Jacuzzi, and a four poster bed with the best mattress money could buy.

"You like it?" I asked.

She walked around, nodding tearfully, and plopped down in a chair. "Yeah. It's nice. Thank you. I just didn't expect any restrictions. What am I going to do all day?"

I could think of a few things I'd like to see her do...

"What do you normally do with your days? Do you have a hobby?"

She considered my question. "Yeah. I do. I'm an artist, remember? I teach, I take classes. That sort of thing." She gave a little laugh, and I thought back to our conversation at the Venetian bar.

A lot had happened since then.

"We'll get you art supplies, then. Make a list of what you'd like and I'll send someone out."

I looked at my watch and realized I needed to go. Although I'd been up all night just like Rain had, and I was equally exhausted, I did not have the benefit of catching up on my sleep. I had a shit ton of work to do, and I knew Dom and Colt were waiting for me, most likely impatiently.

I turned to Rain, who looked like she was moments away from falling asleep.

"The housekeeper will be by shortly with something to eat. Please don't try anything stupid. Your sister's life depends on you right now. Don't forget that."

CHAPTER 9

NICO

"Okay, guys. What do we know?" I asked Dom and Colt as I settled in behind my desk.

They sat back in their chairs and looked at each other. I took that to mean there wasn't any good news. At least not yet. I was normally a patient man, but since I'd seen up close what the abduction of her sister was doing to Rain, I had a slightly new perspective. And it was anything but patient.

"We've not gotten a hell of a lot since you offed our top informant in the basement of the Venetian hotel. With a witness, I might add," Colt said.

That was a loss for us. A big loss.

I nodded. No sense in arguing the point. "Yeah. That was unfortunate. But he was armed and the situation had gotten out of control."

It actually fucking sucked. 'Dan,' or whatever his name was, could have provided us a lot of good information about the trafficking ring we were looking to intercept.

"Anyway," Colt continued, "we did manage to get our hands on some video surveillance from the hotel, and it looks like the girl was definitely taken."

Dom shook his head sadly. "Yeah. It was her. I could tell the moment I saw Rain. They look exactly alike."

"Fuck," I said, putting my head in my hands as a massive headache brewed behind my eyes. "I need to tell Rain it's been confirmed. What do you think the chances are of getting her sister back?"

I looked from Dom to Colt, two guys I'd been best friends with since our Brooklyn childhood. We'd been through the ringer together, and had recently followed our other partner, Leo, here after we closed our New York card club. We each had our own reasons for coming to Vegas, but the common thread was that we all needed a change.

In some ways, I thought this place was even crazier than the Big Apple. Vegas was *about* craziness. There was just no *normal* here.

Some days that was great. Some days it wasn't.

"Nico, you know the chances of finding someone once they're gone. It takes two days, three tops, to get the girl out of the country. Once that happens, she's as good as gone forever. Unless we manage to get some good intel. And now with our guy gone, I honestly don't know the chances of that happening," Colt explained.

"Shit. What else do we have going on?" I asked.

"There's been a string of robberies at pawn shops around town, including one of ours. We're pretty sure we know who's doing it," Dom said. "Bunch of fucking fools if you ask me, thinking they could get away with something like that."

We were all silent for a moment, until Dom steered the conversation in a direction I knew it would eventually go.

"So, Rain. She looked a little worse for the wear, but shit man, she's beautiful. That long, thick hair, shapely legs, and an ass to die for."

"She is beautiful," I said, nodding. "But guys, she's a witness. I'm not sure yet what we should do with her. I made a deal with her."

Dom and Colt looked at each other and smiled.

"Not that kind of deal, you assholes. I told her she had to stick around or we wouldn't look for her sister. That should keep her from running off while we figure out what to do with her."

Dom nodded. "Good thinking."

"I'm surprised they didn't take her as well as her sister. I bet they would have liked to," Colt said. "They may be looking for her, you know. Two pretty sisters? Better than a Vegas jackpot."

I didn't need to be reminded of that.

I stood. "Well, it's time to go tell Rain the bad news. I don't want to keep it from her."

But I didn't want to tell her, either.

I stuffed my hands in my pockets as I headed over to the Agave cottage. I wanted to find Rain's sister. I really did. I didn't want any woman to be subject to the fucked up world of trafficking. But I was especially interested in this case, in part because of the way Rain felt responsible for her sister. I had a feeling if we didn't get Mazzy back, that would kill Rain. Just kill her.

I'd never been so close to a trafficking case before. It sure changed one's perspective.

I knocked lightly on the cottage door. When there was no answer, I quietly let myself in using my key. There was a tray of food the housekeeper had brought over, and I could see Rain had taken a few bites of a sandwich and eaten an apple.

But the place was dead quiet.

So I stuck my head into the bedroom where she was tucked under a thick comforter, breathing steadily. Her clothes from the night before were in a dirty pile, and the wet towels on the floor indicated she'd showered before jumping in bed.

God, she was beautiful, lying there, so innocent and unknowing in her sleep. I didn't want wakefulness to steal that away from her. I could return later.

As I turned to go, she flipped over in bed, partially kicking the covers off.

She had worn nothing to bed, and her movement exposed her breasts.

Christ, I was a fucking perv, to be watching a woman I hardly knew sleep. But that didn't stop me from taking two more steps toward her for a closer look.

Her breasts were small and perky, with pointed dark nipples I was dying to put my mouth on—

"What are you doing?" she shrieked, pulling the covers up to her neck.

Shit, she'd scared me, too.

"Sorry, Rain. I came by to talk to you, but you looked so peaceful I couldn't help but watch you for a minute."

"Well, that's weird. You can leave now," she said, waving me away.

Instead, I took a seat on the edge of the bed and looked around the room with its loveseat and cushy chair in one corner and a mirrored vanity in the other. I hoped she'd be comfortable.

Because she wasn't going anywhere for a while.

CHAPTER 10

RAIN

I was butt naked under the sheets in my prison-slash-cottage, and Nico had just wandered in like he owned the place.

Which, I guess, he did.

But he'd also stood there and watched me, like some kind of damn perv.

And now he'd helped himself to a seat at the end of my bed. "The housekeeper brought you some clothes to wear. We'll take you shopping soon."

I grabbed at the blue GAP shopping bag next to my bed, grateful I wouldn't have to wear my tattered party dress any longer. Turned out that murder, stealing, and kidnapping were hard on a garment.

I pulled out a pair of jeans, a T-shirt, some flip flops,

and undies. I wouldn't win any fashion awards, but it was better than going naked.

Then there was Nico, who had changed out of his expensive Burberry suit of the night before into what looked like an identical one, just a slightly different shade of dark blue.

Boring.

"Thank you," I said, waiting for him to leave so I could dress. "And I don't need you to take me shopping. I have money of my own."

He crossed his arms. "Unless you have a shit ton of cash, you'll need me to take you shopping. Any use of your credit cards will make you easier to find. These trafficking operations are very sophisticated, and since you saw the guy who recruited your sister, they definitely want you now, too."

Had someone just punched me in the stomach? Because it sure felt like it. I rested my head back on the pillow and closed my eyes.

"My god," I whispered. "What a fucking nightmare."

I hadn't wanted to come to Vegas, but Mazzy had insisted we join my friends from art school for one of their twenty-fifth birthdays. In spite of myself, I'd had a decent time up until when the birthday girl started whooping it up, dancing on a table. When the bouncer told her to get down, she'd lifted her dress and given him an up-close beaver shot. Given that we were in Vegas, guys like him probably saw shit like that all the time. He'd rolled his eyes, and when he grabbed her wrist to move her off the table, she'd jumped on him.

And this was the quiet girl.

So we all got kicked out. It was after two a.m., and Mazzy and I decided it was time to turn in anyway. We said our goodbyes to the other three girls—they had an early flight and my sister and I were staying on for another day.

They stumbled off to look for another place to drink, at least until they got kicked out again, or it was time to go to the airport. Whichever came first.

Along came our Uber ride, and the minute we got in, the driver started working us.

"You two ladies are the most beautiful passengers I've picked up all night. No, scratch that. All *week*."

Gee thanks, bud.

"Whatcha girls in town for?"

Mazzy leaned over the seat and began to chat him up. I nudged her at one point to stop flirting, but she blew me off with a dirty look.

"I'm off the clock after this ride. Either of you ladies care to join me for a drink?"

And that was where it all began.

He and Mazzy had headed to the hotel bar, and I went to our room to get ready for bed. But before I knew it, the two joined me, cocktails in hand, kissing and making their way to the bed.

That was when I'd grabbed my shoes and purse and headed for the elevator. Where I met Nico.

"How could we have known the guy Mazzy picked up was bad news? Was there a sign we should have known about? He seemed so... average."

Nico shook his head. "That's the thing. They pick Regular Joe types, so you don't suspect anything. Uber drivers pick up pretty drunk girls all day long in Vegas and know where they're staying. Your sister fell right into their trap. He probably got paid a shit ton of money for finding her, and he'll probably do it again."

It was my fault. I never should have left her alone with him.

As if he'd read my mind, Nico said, "There was nothing you could have done. Once they have you as an easy mark, chances of escape are slim."

God, I just wanted to go back in time twenty-four hours. *Please, universe, please?*

"So what have you heard? Do you know any more about her? And what about picking up our stuff from the room? It's paid for through tomorrow."

Nico looked away from me, and I knew it was bad.

"She was picked up by the traffickers, for certain. We've confirmed that. Now, we're trying to find out if she's still in the country."

My hand flew to my mouth. Why couldn't it have just been me?

I choked back a sob. I was tired of crying. I wanted to get *angry* and *do* something. "Is there any way to negotiate with them? I have money. My family has money. We can pay."

"It's always possible. I was going to bring that up. I know who your father is."

What? Was this guy a mind reader, too?

"How?"

"I got a look at your license when I got your purse back from the trafficker. I made a couple calls when you were napping."

What an asshole.

"You could have just asked me, you know," I fumed.

He gave me a smile I would have liked to smack off his face. "Sorry, Rain. I need to know what I'm dealing with here. Lives are at stake."

He had a point. But still.

"What about getting our stuff?" I asked.

"We're going to keep the room. We paid for it in cash for another week. We think if we leave your stuff there, they'll be watching for you to come back. That's when we can make a move on them."

A fucking nightmare, that's what I was in the middle of.

"When will we know more about Mazzy?"

This was going to kill my mother. Just kill her.

Nico looked my way just in time to catch me wiping tears with the back of my hand. "I know it sucks, Rain. We're going to do everything we can."

His kind words loosened the water works, and my shoulders started to heave. Again.

And then he did something I didn't expect. He

kicked off his shoes and lay down next to me, on top of the covers.

Presumptuous, but under the circumstances, I could feel his concern for me.

And I liked it.

With his head on the pillow and his face inches from mine, he didn't say a thing—he just brushed one of my tears away with his thumb.

So, he *was* human, after all.

Dammit. It was hard to hate him. Or even dislike him. The tiniest bit.

And then I did something surprising. I leaned toward him and pressed my lips to his. It was different than the kiss he'd forced on me earlier. This one was soft and slow and by some miracle lessened my pain, if only for a moment.

He pulled back before I did. "I need to go."

Oh. Well.

But before he did, he stroked my hair, then stopped, like he wanted to say something.

But he didn't.

There was a knock on the cottage door.

"Who is it?" He popped up and put his shoes on, leaving me feeling like an idiot for kissing my captor. What had I been thinking?

Wait. I hadn't been thinking.

I was about to follow him when I realized I still wasn't dressed. Oops.

"Hi. Come in," I heard him say while I yanked my GAP clothes on.

He called to me from the living room. "It's the housekeeper, Clare. I'll see you later, Rain."

And he was gone.

"I'll be right out," I called. "I'm just throwing on these clothes you brought me."

When I was presentable, I found Clare cleaning up my lunch from earlier.

Or had that been breakfast? My internal clock was completely out of whack.

"Thank you for the food, Clare. And for the clothes."

She smiled at me. "You're welcome, Rain. Anything I can do to make you comfortable?"

I grabbed a half sandwich off the tray she was about to take away. "Clare, what's with this place? What's going on?"

She knit her brow. "I'm not sure what you mean."

Hmmm. She knew exactly what I meant.

"I'm not allowed to leave this cottage. Don't you think that's strange?" I asked.

Her expression went blank. She was well trained. "Do what they ask. They are all nice men."

"Clare, nice men don't imprison people."

She shrugged with a small smile and left with that morning's tray of food.

I settled into the overstuff sofa and nibbled on the sandwich I'd swiped.

CHAPTER 11

RAIN

I WASN'T DONE SNACKING when someone else knocked on the door. Cripes, the Agave Cottage was a busy place. Looked like I wasn't going to have to worry about being bored. Or lonely.

"I'm Smitt," a hulk of a man said, standing in the doorway.

"Hi," I replied.

Was I supposed to shake hands with these people, my captors?

He handed me two shopping bags, stepped away, and returned with an easel. A very nice easel.

"My art supplies!" I cried. For a moment, it seemed like everything would be all right. Or at least a little less horrible. "How'd you know what to get me?"

"The guys have their sources."

I rummaged through the bags. "Thank you. This is awesome."

He pressed his lips together and nodded. "You ready to go shopping?"

This place was one surprise after another.

"Shopping?" I asked. All I could think about was painting. The smell and feel of the oils would help transport me to my happy place, god willing.

"Nico asked me to take you to one of the boutiques he and his business partners own. Are those the only clothes you have with you?" he asked, pointing at what I was wearing.

Just then a text came in on my phone.

go with smitt. choose something to wear to dinner tonight. will pick you up at seven

"How'd Nico know my number?" I asked. "He just texted me."

Smitt shrugged.

There was a lot of shrugging going around.

"I thought you'd said I couldn't leave the cottage," I said to Nico after we'd settled into a private booth at Delmonico's.

I reached for the glass of champagne that had been waiting on the table, freshly poured.

He hadn't stopped staring at me since he'd picked me up.

I looked nice. Not fashion-model nice, but still nice.

The boutique Smitt had taken me to was one of the nicest I'd ever been to, and I'd been to some nice freaking stores in my lifetime.

While there, Smitt had taken a seat on an oversized chair where a couple other men waited, and an elegant sales lady whisked me to a private dressing room. There was already a rack full of clothes waiting for me.

"Mr. Nico gave me an idea of what to choose for you, and I guessed at your size. Do you want to flip through these things and let me know what you'd like?"

What a shop.

I glanced through the rack. Wow. He'd somehow figured out what I wore down to the shades of grey and pink I loved. Impressive. "I'll take everything," I said, pulling out my credit card.

She held her hand up. "This is going on Mr. Nico's account. He told me not to take any of your cards."

Guess he hadn't been kidding.

"We'll have everything delivered to the house."

Whatever.

It had been a quick shopping spree, all things considered.

Of course he'd gotten us the best table in the restaurant. Only the best for his prisoner, I supposed.

"Nico? Nico, are you okay?" I asked, waving my

champagne glass in front of him and trying to ignore his dimples and piercing eyes.

Damn him.

He snapped his head back. "Yeah. Sorry. You busted me. I'm blown away by how lovely you are."

Ugh. Not in the mood for anyone's cheesiness.

Falling for a guy's compliments was what got my vain little sister into the horrible place she was in. I wasn't going to fall for it, too. I was there, hanging out with Nico, for one reason and one reason only.

To find Mazzy.

It was that simple. It was a deal I made, not that I had much choice. Did I have to remind him of that?

Actually, I had to remind myself of that.

"Thanks," I said, offhandedly.

I ordered the scallops. I had no idea what he ordered. I wasn't paying attention.

Until he forced me to.

I reached for a piece of the bread the restaurant was famous for, and Nico grabbed my wrist.

Hard.

"That hurts."

He tilted his head and smiled. "Good. Now I've got your attention."

I took a deep breath. Stay calm. Don't be a snarky bitch.

Just when I *most* wanted to be a snarky bitch, I had to suck it up. Life was like that.

"I want to make sure you understand our *deal*."

His grip on my wrist squeezed until my hand began to feel numb. I tried to jerk it away, but of course that only made him hold me tighter.

And even though I was there pretty much against my will, eating with my captor in the clothes he'd bought me at a restaurant he'd chosen, it wasn't lost on me that across the table was probably the most handsome man I'd ever seen.

It wasn't fair.

And now, with tensions rising, I was feeling a little warm *down there*. I crossed and uncrossed my legs to shake off the throbbing.

It did no good.

Nico continued, his dark eyes somehow getting darker.

Was he... excited, like I was?

God, this was fucked up.

"As long as you stick with our deal, we will continue to look for your sister. If you take off, you're on your own."

"You're. Hurting. My. Wrist."

He let me go, and I rubbed where he'd left a red mark.

"That's not fair. I'm just going to call the police," I said.

He took a swig of his champagne and shrugged. "It's not fair. It's also not fair that the police do not have the resources we do. But that's how it is."

My sister's predicament aside, I was made dizzy by

his resolute confidence. He was as certain about what he was saying as the sky was blue.

And I believed him. I wanted my sister back.

"I'm in. The deal is on."

Like I had a choice.

CHAPTER 12

NICO

GOD, this woman was frustrating as hell.

And also fucking gorgeous.

I'd been sporting wood since I'd picked her up for dinner. She was in a jumpsuit cut just low enough to give me an eyeful of her pert little breasts and rock-hard nipples. Now that I was seated directly across from her, I watched her long hair brush the tops of those luscious tits, which bounced the smallest bit every time she raised her champagne to her lips.

Fuck me.

"What's your story?" I asked her.

Surprise washed over her face, but she picked up her fork anyway, as we dove into our shared dessert. "What do you mean?"

She knew what I meant. But good for her for testing me.

"Why are you a rich girl pretending to be a poor girl?"

Her forked slipped from her hand, clattering to the plate below. A server flew around the corner to see what had happened.

"We're fine, thank you," I said, waving him away.

"What the hell are you talking about?" she said in a shaky voice.

I pretty much knew her story—I just wanted to see if I could get her to be honest with me.

So I waited.

She righted her fork. "I don't feel I can be a respected artist if people think my family money paid for my opportunities. So, I live modestly. I'm fine with it. In fact, I enjoy it. My sister does, too. Or did."

She pressed her lips together tightly.

"It's easy to do that when you know you have family money to fall back on, isn't it?"

A shadow passed over her face. "I am an *artist*, remember? You're the one who made me shout it from the mountaintops. Don't look at me like I'm a dilettante, because I'm not."

I called the waiter over for the check. "Didn't say that."

"The art world is very competitive, and people are prone to gossip. I don't need them talking about me, so I keep my head down and work hard."

"And pretend you're not the heir to your father's vast shipping fortune?" I added.

Rolling her eyes, she shrugged. "So, what's *your* story?" she asked when we settled into the car for Smitt to drive us home.

Smitt, the all-around security guy, driver, sounding board, and chief of staff. The dude got paid a fuck load of money, and he earned every penny of it. I don't know what I ever did without him.

My fingers stroked the silk crepe of Rain's jumpsuit when she reached for my hand.

Yeah. She reached for my hand.

"I grew up in Brooklyn with Dom and Colt. We come from *family businesses*, if you know what I mean."

She shook her head. "I don't know. What does that mean?"

"Our dads and uncles were all in business together. And now we're in business together."

As we drove out of the city, and street lights ceased to exist, Rain's lovely face was shadowed so I could only see her glittering eyes.

I wanted to see her face again.

Damn, I was a pussy.

"My grandfather imported olive oil from Italy. As that business grew, he got into trucking and distribution. He got a lot of business from people he knew and was very successful."

She didn't need to know much more than that. Although she'd ask again. I knew she would.

Smitt dropped us at the door to her cottage.

"So, you're gonna lock me in?" she asked with a sly smile. "I am a prisoner, after all, right?"

Damn if she wasn't flirting with me.

"You know it. But not before I come in and properly thank you for joining me for dinner," I said, opening her door with my key.

I followed her in, my eyes glued to the upside down heart that was her ass, silk clinging just enough to show off the tiny jiggle of her ass cheeks.

She sat on the sofa, where I joined her.

"*I* am the one who should be thanking *you*," she said.

Fuck.

I leaned toward her and pressed my lips to the side of her neck, dragging them from her earlobe to the crook of her neck and back. She sighed quietly, and I ran a hand up her bare arm, past her shoulder, to her cheek, and pulled her to me for a kiss.

Our lips lingered as if meeting for the first time, a sort of magic I knew was hard to come by. I couldn't explain it and certainly didn't understand it. But I'd never forget it.

As if we were thinking the same thing, our kiss became more urgent, perhaps to leave behind some of the bullshit we both carried. I let my hand fall down to her breast, kneading her flesh through the black silk she was wearing.

Reaching behind her neck, she untied the halter top of her jumpsuit, and the fabric that had loosely covered her breasts fell away. I pulled back to appreciate her beautiful tits, firm and upturned with puffy brown nipples.

I put my hands on her small waist and pulled her to stand with me.

She started to kick off her high heels.

"Keep them on. I like them."

My weakness. Well, one of them, anyway. *Fuck me* shoes.

Her arms met at the back of my neck, and she tilted her head to press her lips to mine again. While she did, I found the zipper for her outfit on the side of her pants. I opened it and my beautiful girl stood before me in nothing more than a lacy thong and skyscraper heels.

I was so hard I was in agony. I stepped back to take her in.

"Fuck, you're beautiful," I growled.

I had to taste her. Couldn't wait a moment longer.

"Take off your thong. Then sit." I gestured at the couch.

Her gaze locked with mine, she hooked her thumbs in the waistband of her panties, and slowly, slowly, slipped them over her smooth hips, stepping out of them with careful balance. Standing back up, she was both defiant and shy in her nakedness, her hands fidgeting until she calmed. After all, *I* was still fully dressed.

And what a vision she was with her smooth, flawless skin, and hair cascading over her shoulders like a goddamn Lady Godiva.

"Open your legs," I said, once she sat down.

She looked up at me with a sly smile and placed her hands on her thighs. Bit by bit, she parted her knees.

"More."

I finally had my first view of her glorious pussy, shaved and smooth like the rest of her glowing skin, slightly opened by the angle of her parted legs.

"Touch yourself."

She hesitated for a split second and then confidence set in. One hand wandered down to her slit while the other drifted over her belly and breasts.

When she pulled open her lips, I could see her most intimate parts, pink and glistening with her excitement. Her clit stood like a hard nub, which she circled and then settled on, rubbing until her head fell back on the sofa and her eyes closed.

To say I was looking at the most beautiful sight I'd ever seen was an understatement. I was nearly frozen in place like the fool that I was, until a small moan escaped her lips and pulled me out of my reverie. I threw my suit jacket aside and knelt, my face level with her sex.

Placing my thumbs on either side of her lips, I gently opened her, dying to see and consume what was before me.

Her fingers tangled in my hair as she pulled me closer.

I pressed my nose into her to gulp her scent and flicked her with my tongue. She was sweet and delicious, like I knew she'd be. I ran up and down through her folds, lapping her juices from clit to ass and back as if I were a starving man. She squirmed and writhed under my touch, her breath coming in short, tight gasps.

"Oh my god, Nico," she murmured.

"You're so good, baby. You taste so fucking good."

As she grew closer to orgasm, I opened my trousers with one hand and pulled my cock out through a tangle of shirttails and boxers. I stroked myself slowly so I didn't explode like a teenage boy, because damn if I wasn't aching to pummel her. But there'd be time for that later.

Her sighs turned to moans, and just when she was on the edge, she began to scream and thrash.

"I'm coming... I'm coming!" she cried.

As soon as her first orgasm rolled over her and she started catching her breath, I pushed myself to my feet. When she saw my hard cock in hand, she smiled. "Come for me."

That was all it took. One more stroke, and I exploded onto her tits.

"Fuck!" I roared.

She smiled at me beatifically, rubbing my cum into her skin.

I sank into the sofa and pulled her into my lap.

Goddamn, what this woman did to me. It was frightening.

And dangerous.

CHAPTER 13

NICO

"HEY GUYS," I said as Dom and Colt entered my office and made themselves at home. "Give me the news."

Colt rubbed his hand over his bald head and leaned forward in his seat. "She's gone."

Something jabbed the pit of my stomach. I wasn't normally this engaged with trafficking victims, but things were different now. And it didn't feel good.

"It looks like they took her out of the country yesterday," he continued. "But none of our connections know where she was taken."

I realized I was gripping the edges of my desk when my hands started to ache.

"When we find them, those guys are so fucking dead—"

Colt held his hands up. "Slow down, cowboy. Let's wait until we find the girl. Otherwise, she might be lost forever."

"Yeah, yeah. I know that. Listen, guys, let's not share any of this with Rain yet. It's gonna crush her. If not kill her."

"Sounds like the two of you are getting pretty cozy, huh?" Colt asked with a smirk.

I rolled my eyes. "Fuck off, asshole."

I was busted. And I didn't give a shit.

"Next order of business," Dom said. "We have a meeting set up with the Matteo family at Luca and Leo's request. Since the brothers learned that Sal took out their mother, it's looking like he may have had something to do with their father's disappearance, too."

"Damn. Federico Borroni disappeared when Luca and Leo were barely teenagers. Do you think he's still alive?" I asked.

Dom shrugged. "It's possible. You never know. But it would do the guys a world of good to at least know what happened to him. Even if he's been dead all these years."

That was some crazy shit. One day, when Luca and Leo were in their teens, their dad didn't show up for dinner. He didn't show up the next night, either.

He was gone, without a trace.

"Well, take it slow with Sal's guys," I said. "If we get rid of them outright, we'll never find out what happened to the Borroni's father. But you know, feel free to apply a little *pressure* if that would help."

"I'll fucking torture them without mercy if they think they're gonna be smart asses," Colt said, his face turning red.

Yeah, he was the hothead of the group.

"All right, guys. Hit the road. See what you can find out about Borroni, and also let me know the second you get word about Rain's sister."

I went up to my bedroom stretching and yawning. I didn't want to let on to the guys, but after my hot session with Rain, I'd not been able to sleep all night. I'd come back home even though she'd invited me to spend the night, but damn if I didn't just toss and turn.

She'd slept like a baby, though. How did I know that?

I watched her half the goddamn night from my bedroom window.

Creepy? I didn't give a shit.

And walking over to the window now, I could see she'd set up her easel and paints. Wearing baggy jeans, she was braless under a loose tank top, and was making wide, graceful strokes across one of the canvasses Smitt had picked up for her. Every couple minutes, she'd take a step back and look at her work, either smiling approvingly or shaking her head in dissatisfaction.

She was lost in her work, wrapped up in a different world, one where nothing bad had happened to either

her or her sister, and I was envious. I had nothing like that to take me away from my daily grind.

Although the night before, when we were enjoying each other—that had been pretty transcendent. I'd be lying if I didn't admit all was right in the world during the time we were together.

There'd be more of that. I knew it.

CHAPTER 14

RAIN

EVEN THOUGH I had my paints, I still chafed at being locked up in a damn cottage. It didn't matter how many pretty clothes or nice meals Nico treated me to—no one wants to be a prisoner.

Thank god they'd gotten me some oils to take my mind off things.

But I couldn't paint twelve hours a day.

And I was seriously locked in. I'd tried the front and back doors to the cottage, but no luck. I could bust through a window, of course, if I were desperate. And I *was* getting desperate. If I didn't get something definitive about my sister soon, I'd have to come clean to my parents. As it was, I'd told them we'd decided to stay on in Vegas to do some more touristy things, like go hiking.

We never hiked, but they'd bought it. Thank god.

I couldn't keep putting them off. It wasn't right. They deserved to know what had happened to Mazzy. They had money and resources. They'd work with the police to make things happen. Even though Nico had said that was useless.

In the news you heard all the time about trafficked people being rescued.

Right?

Okay, maybe not.

But still. It seemed insane not to involve the authorities, and I was getting more and more uncomfortable with that concept every day, in part because I'd not heard a word from Nico. We'd had an insane sexy session after our dinner out, and since then... crickets. Nice guy. Get some nookie, move on.

What the hell did I expect? He and his buddies were thugs, there were no two ways about it. Dude wasn't exactly Prince Charming.

With a knock on my door, Clare entered with a tray of sandwiches and salads. I had to hand it to her, she went all out making sure I got something I liked.

Better treatment than most prisoners got, I figured.

"Do you mind if I straighten up a bit while I'm here?" she asked.

"Of course not, please go right ahead."

Yeah. Go ahead.

I had somewhere to go.

Good old Clare hadn't locked the door behind

herself when she came in. I grabbed my purse and the keys she'd left next to my tray of food and slipped out the door quietly.

Locking it behind myself, of course. Clare was now stuck in the cottage, and I was free.

I'd apologize later.

I wasn't completely free, however, because the huge iron gate across the drive did not look like something anyone but Spiderman could get over.

Shit.

I ducked behind an outbuilding when I saw a car coming up the drive. The gate swung open and Colt drove in. He leaned out the car window to talk to the guard, who then ran around the side of the car and jumped in. The gate closed and they drove further into the compound, leaving the guard house empty.

Waiting until they were out of sight, I dashed to the little building.

Shit. It was locked. So I wrapped my jacket around my arm, turned away from the door with closed eyes, and rammed my elbow through the glass.

Victory. I reached inside the door and let myself in. In seconds, I'd found the button to open the gate, and I was free.

I was freaking terrified. Nico and the guys had been nice to me up 'til now, aside from locking me in my luxury prison. But who knew how far I could push them until they got really pissed? And who knew what they would do when they reached their limit?

I jogged down the street until I reached another house. I crouched behind some bushes to stay out of sight, and called a cab.

Yeah, I was done with ride-share services.

Did these guys have any idea their oh-so-tight security systems couldn't keep me locked up? They were going to be pissed when they figured it out. But that wasn't my problem. My sister, however, *was*.

I was going back to the Venetian to see what I could learn.

The cab, which had come in minutes, dropped me a block from the hotel, as I'd requested.

I ran up to the side of the Venetian and around to the front and slipped in without the bellmen noticing. With my head down, I hustled toward the bank of elevators to the tower our room was in.

I pulled out the card key that had been tucked in my purse since that awful night and flashed it against the elevator card reader.

It still worked.

I stepped all the way to the back of the elevator to avoid attracting any attention, and when I arrived at my floor, pushed through the crowd with my head down.

My heart was racing. All I wanted to do was curl up in a corner and close my eyes. I'd run off from Nico's estate without much of a plan in mind, and I still wasn't sure what I was doing, except that I was moving toward the place where I'd last seen my sister.

I could just picture how pissed Nico was going to be when he found out I'd gone AWOL. But to be honest, I was sure he'd figure I'd head back to the hotel. Which meant I had to work quickly. He would not be far behind.

The hallway was silent except for a vacuum running in the distance. I slipped my card key into the slot next to the door, and *boom*, a green light activated. I was in.

Oh my god. I was in the room where I'd left my sister. What was crazy, and kind of creepy, was that it looked like she'd been there only minutes before, with things strewn about as Mazzy had no doubt fought off her captor. Everything else was the same, down to the wine glasses she and her 'friend' had brought with them.

Nico had the room paid for, but also made sure housekeeping stayed out. How did you even make something like that happen?

The elevator bell dinged in the distance, and voices approached the room. Jesus, Nico had been fast. Just to be a pain in the ass, I ducked into one of the closets behind the hanging clothes Mazzy and I had left behind. The smell of my sister's perfume on them gave me a lump in my throat that I forced myself to swallow away.

And just as I expected, the lock on the door clicked, and heavy footsteps walked in.

CHAPTER 15

RAIN

"WHY'D we have to come back here again? This is such a waste of time," a male voice said.

Oh god.

That wasn't Nico's voice. Or Dom's or Colt's.

The bedsprings squeaked as someone took a seat.

"Seriously," a different male voice said. "It seems silly, but they want us checking to see if she comes back looking for her sister."

Oh my god. Who were these guys?

I slowed my breathing to calm my racing pulse, the terror running through my veins making me dizzy and clouding my thoughts.

Stay calm, breathe....

"Well, looks like the bitch hasn't been back."

One of them rummaged through our suitcases.

"Dude, look at these hot thongs. God, I'd love to have a few minutes with one of these girls. You saw the one we got. She was fucking beautiful, and her sister was apparently just as pretty."

Nausea rose in my throat. I swallowed, hoping the sensation would pass.

But it only got worse.

"Yeah man, the first one they got, she's already in fucking Thailand, I heard. Probably will be sold off to some pervy old dude in the middle east or something."

At that news, I had to clamp a hand over my mouth.

My sister? Thailand? The Middle East?

Oh god. What would I tell my parents?

"Let's head out. She hasn't been here. Look at everything. Exactly the same as last time we checked. Even that toothbrush with the toothpaste on it is still on the bathroom sink."

Footsteps headed toward the door. "I'd like to stay in a joint like this some day. The Venetian is the balls."

"Keep doing what you're doing, dude, and the money will come. You've seen the boss. He hooks you up if you deliver."

The door clicked shut behind them, and I sank to the floor of the closet. I wanted to scream and cry and rail, but it wasn't the time.

Although I did jump up and reach the toilet just in time to vomit.

I ran around the room in a panic. I didn't know

what to do. I absolutely could not come up with a single idea.

Nico.

He would eventually find me. I might as well make it easier for him.

"Where the fuck are you?" he growled over the phone.

Strangely, even though he was clearly angry, the sound of his voice was soothing. Defying all logic, the man made me feel safe.

And sexy. And beautiful.

But now was not the time for that.

"Oh, Nico—"

These were the only words I could get out before my sobs took away my ability to speak, and my horror took away my ability to think straight.

"Are you at the hotel?" he asked.

"Ye... yes," I cried.

"I'll be there in fifteen."

Like a scared little kid, I crawled back in the closet. All I knew was I wanted to regress to some point in time where I didn't have to act like a grown up, when some adult could make it all better. But when I crawled as far inside as I could and buried my face in my sister's clothes, I knew there was no one to rescue me. I was going to have to rescue myself and my sister.

After what felt like an hour later, the hotel door opened again and heavy male steps made their way across the room, checking in the bathroom and all corners. I cowered in the closet and reminded myself to *breathe*.

"Rain?" Nico called.

"Oh my god," I said, rushing out of the closet and into his arms.

I knew I was going to be in all sorts of trouble, but at the moment, I just needed to feel safe. Desperately.

"They were here, Nico, the traffickers were here. They said my sister's in Thailand. We have to get her. Nico, please say you'll help me."

"They were just here?" he asked, running his hand over his hip. Was that to check on his gun?

I nodded, my mind racing.

How fast could I get to Thailand?

I had to find her. I had to.

"Okay, Rain. Calm down. Now," he said, putting his hands on either side of my face and squeezing lightly.

"Uh... um... "

"You shouldn't be here. You know how lucky you are they didn't look in the closet for you? They clearly sent the newbies out to do the job, because anyone else would have turned the place upside down. And they would have found you, and you would probably be wearing a blindfold and gag, on your way to a private airstrip somewhere. They'd have you out of the country by morning."

I was shaking so hard I couldn't form any words. Nico pulled me down to the edge of the bed, with his arms around me.

"I'm pissed at you for taking off like that, Rain. You broke our deal. I'm tempted to say, *see ya*, and let you figure out what to do with your sister on your own."

Not surprisingly, I found my voice. "No! No, no no. You can't do that." I grabbed his lapels. "Please, Nico. I'm sorry I ran off, but I couldn't stand sitting around any longer. I just kept thinking about what my sister might be going through, and I was losing my mind. It was torture."

I let go of him, and my shoulders slumped. "It still is torture. Who knows what those evil people are doing with her."

I put my hands over my face.

"C'mon, Rain. We have to get the hell out of here. Who knows when those fuckers are coming back, and next time they might send some guys with brains."

He pulled me to my feet and looked around the room. "Grab whatever you want."

"B... but don't we want to make it look like we were never here?"

He threw a suitcase on the bed and started throwing things in it. "Get moving. And to answer your question, we *want* them to know we've been here. It's time to fuck with them. Draw them out. It may be our only hope."

CHAPTER 16

NICO

DAMN WOMAN.

She was lucky I liked her. Anybody else I would have cut loose without a second thought. As it was, if she didn't wise up, I wouldn't be looking only for her sister—I'd be looking for her, too.

She had no idea how close her foolish risk had just brought her to meeting the same fate as Mazzy, and to think she'd been mere inches away from being taken made my head pound. If those idiots had thought to open the closet door, Rain might have been halfway around the world already.

What an unnecessary waste that would have been.

I understood why she'd done it, but if she'd been caught by the traffickers herself, she'd be of no use to her sister.

When I first got word that she'd escaped the compound, a sense of dread unlike anything I'd ever experienced washed over me. It was completely unexpected. I barely knew the woman. Such a reaction seemed so overblown—disproportionate to the time we'd spent together. Although I *was* getting to know her better... in several important ways.

Hell, that night when I'd eaten her pussy was one of the hottest goddamn experiences I'd ever had—the way she squirmed under me, so out of control and vulnerable but strong and sexy at the same time. I didn't think I'd ever met anyone like her.

And now I was getting a hard-on, dammit. Actually, I'd had a hard-on pretty much since I'd first met her in that elevator at the Venetian.

She wouldn't go anywhere for a while this time. It appeared she'd learned a lesson by getting the shit scared out of her.

Making himself comfortable in my great room, Dom made a drink and propped his feet up on my coffee table. "Hey, Nico, is Clare spitting mad that Rain locked her in the cottage and took off? Seriously. Pulling shit like that on a housekeeper."

It was funny about Clare. She wasn't mad she'd been locked in the cottage per se, but she was furious the cake she'd been baking burned because she wasn't back in time to take it out of the oven.

Don't mess with Clare's cooking. I tried tasting some of her mashed potatoes once and was lucky to have walked away with all ten of my fingers. I'd hired her the moment I arrived in Vegas, and she ran my household like a drill sergeant, keeping me and everything around us on schedule.

"So how'd Rain get out, anyway?" Dom asked.

"I can tell you," Colt interrupted as he joined us. "I asked the guard at the front gate for some help moving a piece of furniture in my house, and she took advantage of the opportunity to split. She must have been waiting. Watching."

We both pivoted to glare at him.

"You know better than to ask the guard to leave his post. What the fuck," Dom said.

But Colt was cocky. Always had been, always would be. I'd been hanging around with the guy since before we were ten years old. He'd never admit to a mistake, nor would he ever apologize.

He shrugged. "Can't blame Rain for taking off. Who the hell wants to be locked up in a cottage?"

Now he was getting under my skin. "You know damn well she's locked up for her safety—and ours."

I braced myself for his smart-ass remarks.

"Somebody likes the new girl," Colt said in a singsong voice.

"Yeah," I said. "I do. What's the big deal? She's pretty and smart. That's it. As soon as we find her sister, we're cutting her loose. She lives in fucking LA. She can't wait to get out of Vegas and get back to her life. We'll never see her again."

She probably hated my goddamn guts, despite the fact that we'd messed around.

Colt leaned forward, stroking his beard, like he always did when he had a point to make. "Speaking of which, Nico, I'm not sure we'll be able to find her sister. Hate to tell you this, but if she landed in Thailand already, god knows where she could be now. Probably in the harem of some Saudi prince." He chuckled.

He was lucky I didn't slug him. Asshole.

"Really funny, Colt. Your compassion is overwhelming."

He rolled his eyes. "You know what I mean, Nico. Just relieving some tension. Seriously, do you actually think we're going to find this woman? It's like looking for a needle in a haystack. She could be anywhere, and you know wherever she is, she's well hidden. You gotta be realistic."

Dom, always a voice of reason, pointed a finger. "But Colt, you have contacts who can help us track her. Where are you with all that?"

Colt leaned back and crossed his legs. "Oh well, yeah, I'm working on it. But I can't get perfect information every time. Are you kidding?"

"Goddammit Colt. Do you remember what happened to the last woman we tried to help?" I asked.

He hung his head.

Good. I wanted him to feel like shit.

Colt had gotten bad information. We'd told the

woman when the coast was clear and that she needed to run. But it wasn't clear after all, and she'd been taken down by a bullet to the back.

That was a bad day. A really bad day. We'd been so close to saving a young woman whose entire life was in front of her.

I still didn't understand how it happened, and I was still broken up about it. We all were. At least I thought so.

But Colt's cavalier attitude was pissing me off.

I leaned forward in my chair for emphasis. "Colt, you need to fucking find her. That's all there is to it," I said through gritted teeth. I set down my drink. "Have a good evening, guys."

I headed over to Rain's cottage. I couldn't wait any longer. I had to be in her company. I didn't like it, but I was drawn to her like a freaking magnet.

Dammit.

CHAPTER 17

NICO

"WHAT ARE YOU WORKING ON?" I asked, checking out the sketches she'd scattered all over the floor at her feet.

They were of a woman. Who looked surprisingly like Rain.

Mazzy.

She scrambled to gather the sheets of drawing paper, but there were so many, she couldn't collect them all before I saw what she'd been doing.

"Nothing. Just messing around with some sketches," she said, tucking everything into a neat pile and placing it face down.

But she hadn't hidden the work on her easel, which pretty much gave it all away.

"That's your sister, Mazzy, isn't it?" I asked.

She shrugged, still avoiding my gaze. "I'm just messing around. No big deal."

"This is good work, Rain. You're really talented."

She took a seat and sighed. "Thanks. I found a picture of Mazzy I really liked on my phone and was working from that."

I sat next to her. "But you didn't want me to see your work. Why?"

She looked down at her paint-stained fingers. "It's something I'm doing for Mazzy. As if by painting her, we'd be connected, and she'd know I was trying to find her. Or at least, that someone was trying to find her. I wanted to see if I could feel her pain. You know, get a sense of her state of mind."

"Heady stuff. Did it work?"

"Nah. Not really," she said, shaking her head.

God, it broke my heart to see how much she cared for her sister, and how hard she was trying, in her own way, to reach out to her.

"I guess I feel *a little* like she's with me," Rain said, turning her sketches right-side-up.

I reached for them. "Can I see?"

She reluctantly passed them over. I wasn't sure why she was guarding them so jealously.

They were beautiful. Simple pencil sketches, but she'd caught the essence of all her sister's moods by showing her smiling, frowning, and lost in thought. And she was stunning, just like her big sister.

I knew Rain had sketched these creations to feel her

sister's presence, but interestingly, looking at them, I felt it, too.

And I wanted to get her back at least at much as Rain did.

But I didn't tell Rain there was a good chance she'd never see her sister again. I should have, to set her expectations, but I just couldn't bear to dash her hopes. She was already suffering so much.

Which made me feel even shittier for locking her up. The only thing on her mind was saving Mazzy. She posed no threat to me or the guys, even though she'd witnessed a murder. She wasn't going anywhere with that information.

"I'm sorry this is happening to you, Rain," I said, pulling her to me.

She sniffled and wiped her eyes with the back of her hand. Lifting her face toward mine, she reached for a kiss.

Well, that was all I needed.

I buried my fingers in her lush hair and pulled her closer. She returned my kiss with an urgency I recognized—one of needing a moment away from the pain. Anything to forget.

I knew how that felt. My heart had been destroyed before, too.

Rain pulled her paint-spattered tank top off over her head and tossed it to the floor. She stood and pushed her baggy jeans down and stepped out of them.

And she was naked.

My girl hadn't been wearing skivvies.

Hot.

I remained fully dressed as she pushed me back on the sofa and straddled me, spreading her legs over my thighs until I could see her beautiful pussy open wide, all pink and glistening.

But I didn't move. I wanted to see what she would do.

Pushing her hips forward, she slipped her fingers between her folds. Rocking right there in my lap, she began to work herself, first sliding her hand through her slick flesh, then burying two fingers.

"Oh, shit," she whispered. "I need this."

Glad to assist.

Bucking her hips, she moved up and down on her fingers in one of the hottest fucking things I'd ever seen.

Her mouth opened slightly, and her eyes closed. Her head dropped to her chest and her hair flew about from her movements.

I couldn't wait any longer.

Like a hungry animal, I ran my hands along her ass cheeks, up her back, and over her shoulders to get to her tits. I tweaked her hard nipples, and she continued to buck, her breath coming harder and faster.

Keeping one hand on her breast, I seized her ass with my other and moved her faster up and down while she fucked herself.

"Oh... oh... I'm coming," she murmured, bucking so hard I had to hold her so she didn't fall off my lap.

What a sight, to watch a beautiful woman bring herself to orgasm right in front of me.

Yeah.

After a moment, her eyes opened, and she slipped off my lap. Kneeling on the floor in front of me, she grabbed for my belt and fly, and got my pants and boxers around my ankles in seconds. My hard dick slapped against my stomach, and I put my hands on her head to direct her.

She started by grabbing me at my base and running her tongue up my length, then back down my shaft. Taking my head, she made circles around it with her tongue, teasing me mercilessly and then pulling me in further, her lips creating the most delicious suction.

It was all I could do to not blow my load right then and there in her pretty mouth. But I wanted my pleasure to last.

How the hell did I go from meeting a beautiful woman in an elevator, to trying to save her sister, to having these insane erotic moments?

She bounced her lips over the rim of my cock head, slowly taking me in her mouth until I was deep in her throat.

Fucking A, she wasn't even gagging. I'd never ever seen anything like it.

To her surprise, I lifted her off me, her mouth

momentarily hanging open in disbelief that I'd interrupted her sexy force.

I laid her face-down on the cottage floor. I grabbed a condom from my trouser pocket and sheathed myself, straddling her ass.

"Open yourself," I growled.

Her hands flew back to her ass cheeks, and she spread herself apart like a blooming flower. I notched myself at her gushing pussy and plunged inside to my balls.

And it was exquisite, the squeeze she had on my cock made that much tighter by our position. She screamed under me, pounding the floor, and I wondered if anyone could hear us outside the cottage.

But to be honest, I didn't care.

With one more thrust so hard she shook, I emptied my painful balls, pumping until I had nothing left.

CHAPTER 18

RAIN

I'D JUST HAD the most cheery call with my parents. My poor parents.

Who had no idea their eldest daughter was a liar of epic proportions. I'd told them breathlessly of all the fun Mazzy and I were having in Vegas between our excursions, spa days, and nightly shows.

If I didn't stop making it sound so good, they'd want to come join us.

I hated lying, especially to them, but I didn't see any benefit to sharing what was really going on—at least, not yet. It would only result in a disaster of epic proportions. They'd want to get the police involved, for starters. My dad—I could just see it—would bring in a private investigator he'd known for years, who knew little or nothing about the world of human trafficking. All well-intended, but if what Nico was saying was right, counter-productive as hell.

All this activity would not bode well for my sister, which was the bottom line for me. And I believed Nico —not that I had any choice. But he knew more about this world than anyone else I knew, and I was willing to follow his lead—to a point. In due time, if I wasn't seeing us getting closer to finding Mazzy, then I'd bring in my dad, who'd recruit the big guns. At that point the chips would fall wherever they did.

They were all, essentially, the best/worst option.

I prayed we wouldn't get to that point. It would be as bad as admitting defeat.

Nico invited me to lunch—or more accurately, informed me we were going to lunch—and I jumped at the invitation. Spending my day—the entire day— locked up in a little cottage was not my idea of fun. I doubted it was anybody's idea of fun, no matter how beautifully outfitted the place was and how many oil paints there were to play with.

How the hell could I reconcile an epic attraction to the sexiest guy who'd ever crossed my path, with the fact that he was essentially keeping me jailed?

Never mind whose safety it was for.

The contradictions gave me whiplash.

I slipped a midi-length wrap dress from Nico's boutique over my head, and when it shimmied over my hips, I smiled at my reflection in the mirror. It fit like a glove, and the orange-red was grabby without being tacky. I pulled on some new high-heeled sling backs, and my outfit was complete.

And no, I was not wearing undies.

A sharp knock fell on my door at exactly noon and a more-handsome-than-ever Nico walked in.

The facial scruff he'd been sporting the past few days was gone, revealing the perfect planes of his masculine face. And then there were those dimples.

Seriously, the universe was having a very good day when it created him.

He was almost too handsome to look at, and even though we'd been intimate, close proximity to him still made me shake with excitement.

And, I supposed, a little fear.

A few minutes later we'd settled into a private corner at another one of Vegas' top restaurants, where, of course, Nico knew everybody.

"Baby, do you mind if I go say hi to the chef over there?" he asked.

"'Course not."

Baby. So I was *baby.*

He bent to kiss my temple, and best of all, I got to watch him walk across the restaurant and observe the heads turning in his wake.

He looked back and damn if he didn't catch me staring.

Busted.

When he'd moved out of my line of sight, I got back

to the menu. Clare's cooking was great, but it was nice to try something different, too. The butter poached sole caught my attention, but it was hard to decide between that and the—

"I was just noticing you sitting alone, Miss, and I wanted to tell you how beautiful you are."

I looked up at a man, tall and thin, and possibly good-looking if not for his pitted complexion and crooked nose.

"Oh, thank you, but—"

I looked around anxiously for Nico.

"Miss, I just wanted to ask for your number. You know, to have coffee sometime."

I didn't want to be a bitch, but someone needed to tell this guy his game was off. You don't pick up a woman on a date. At least not in my world.

"No. Thank you for asking," I said as unambiguously as possible.

He smiled broadly, but his eyes were cold. He looked over his shoulder, trying to be casual. "Oh, c'mon. What's the harm? You might enjoy yourself. I'm a fun guy."

Something felt off.

"I said, *no thank you.*" I smiled politely, hoping he'd take off.

Instead his smile faded, replaced with something I could only call ugly.

Fuck, where was Nico? I craned my neck to see

beyond the man and started to reach for my phone when I saw Nico had left his there on the table. Shit.

The guy leaned closer, lowering his voice. "Fine. Fine, *Rain*. Do you want to see your sister, *Mazzy*, ever again?"

Um, what?

A tsunami of dizziness washed over me, and in spite of my sleeveless outfit, a damp sweat broke out on my temples.

Had he just said something about Mazzy?

"I... I don't... who are you—" I fumbled, my throat getting tighter. "How do you know about... my sister?"

"Look Rain, do you ever want to see your sister again?" he asked.

I tried to stand, but he put his hand on my shoulder so I couldn't budge without attracting attention.

"Wh... where is my sister?" I said through the lump in my throat.

I twisted to see Nico emerge from the kitchen, thank god. But he was still chatting with the chef, and not looking my way.

The man saw me trying to catch Nico's eye. Lifting his hand from my shoulder, he took off as quickly as he'd appeared.

Gone.

Had he been my imagination?

"Hey, baby, sorry about that," Nico said, taking his chair and putting his napkin in his lap in one graceful movement.

"I... I... "

He immediately realized something was up. "Rain. What happened?" He reached for my shaking hand.

I took a gulp of water and filled him in.

His face turned dark with rage. "Wait here. Don't talk to anyone."

He stood, scanned the restaurant, and headed for the front entrance.

I just sat there, shaking and wiping away discreet tears.

Who was that man and how did he know how to find me at lunch? Had he been following me? Did he know where Nico was hiding me?

"Ma'am, are you okay?" the waiter asked, returning with our wine.

But Nico's hand was on my arm, pulling me to my feet. "Thank you, but we need to leave. Family emergency." He pressed some bills into the waiter's hand, and we headed out front to where Smitt was waiting.

"D... did you find anybody?" I asked, my voice trembling as he opened the car door so I could jump in first.

"No. He got away. He either had a car waiting, or he knew how to slip out the back," he said as Smitt hit the road. "Bastards. They'll pay for this."

When we got back to Nico's compound, for the first time he brought me into his house rather than the cottage. I could barely speak and could walk only very stiffly. He put an arm around my shoulder, and I leaned into him.

When had I earned 'house privileges?' I wanted to ask, but was shaking too hard.

While I would have liked to see Nico's place under happier circumstances, in my fog, I was nevertheless blown away by its soaring ceilings, dark wood, and exposed beams. The foyer was massive and reminded me of a mountaintop lodge, just without the stuffed animal heads, thank god—not at all what I'd expected to find in the middle of the desert.

"Clare," he shouted.

The housekeeper appeared immediately, wiping her hands on her apron.

"Yes, Mr. Nico."

"Could you please order us some Chinese food? My usual favorites," he said.

I smiled weakly at her, hoping I was forgiven for locking her in my cottage.

We climbed a wide, curved staircase, and he led me to a sitting room full of bookcases, leather easy chairs, an overstuffed sofa, and a large screen TV.

It was so cozy, I wanted to cry.

"You live here alone, Nico? It's so big," I managed to say.

He led me to the sofa where we he pulled off my shoes and then his own. I followed his lead and put my feet up on the coffee table.

"Yeah. I live here alone. But I wasn't always single. I had a wife back in New York."

Holy shit. I didn't know anything about this guy.

"Divorce?" I asked.

He nodded, his gaze fixed on the TV as he surfed channels.

Well, if that wasn't a hint to ask no more questions, I didn't know what was.

CHAPTER 19

RAIN

AFTER A FEW BITES of the best Chinese food I'd ever had, and watching the classic Hitchcock movie, *Marnie*, I must have dozed off because I woke the next morning, undressed, in Nico's bed with the desert sun blaring through the windows. Even though I'd barely had anything to drink the night before, my head felt stuffed with cotton balls, probably from sleeping too long. Nico was nowhere to be seen, so I stumbled to his bathroom to gulp some tap water.

The house was dead quiet, as I supposed it always was. When I'd quenched my thirst, I grabbed Nico's robe, wrapping myself in its oversized softness. I took the opportunity to poke around his room, tastefully masculine with its dark colors and heavy wooden furniture. Oversized abstract paintings perfectly complemented the staid decor.

Now his interest in my artwork made sense. The man had an eye for art. A good one.

Go figure.

From his window, I discovered that his room overlooked my cottage, and in particular afforded a nice view directly into it.

Yeah, I'm sure *that* was pure coincidence.

Whatever.

I watched the front gate swing open and closed, and a car pulled in, which was greeted by the armed security guard.

The place was busy.

On the other side of the room, I pulled open two French doors and slipped into Nico's vast closet, where I ran my fingers across his starched white dress shirts and dark suits. Everything was perfectly tidy and organized.

What this his doing or the housekeeper's?

I was running my fingers over the top of a cedar dresser when my curiosity got the better of me. I pulled open the top drawer. Inside was a dark, carved box that looked like it might hold watches or cuff links.

I knew that I should probably close the dresser at that point, put my clothes back on, and return to my cottage and figure out how I was going to spend my day, but I just couldn't tear my eyes from the pretty box.

So of course, I lifted the lid.

Inside, it looked like a typical jewelry box, and when I pushed aside some old keys and a tattered rabbit's foot, I pulled out a photo of Nico with a woman who reminded me a bit of myself —similar build with long, highlighted hair like mine.

Then, I pulled out a thick, gold bracelet that definitely didn't belong to any man. On the inside it said:

Our love is forever. Your Nico.

Oh. Shit.

The guy had been through the ringer. Did she leave him? Or the other way around?

Just then, I heard a commotion from downstairs.

Probably just household staff. Right?

Doors opened and slammed and voices got louder, but I couldn't make out what they were saying. I recognized Clare's voice, which was getting loud and shrill. Then she screamed, and I heard the deafening sound of a gun firing.

Just like I'd heard in the hotel.

Holy shit. The terror I'd felt hiding out in the hotel's closet just a couple days before came back with a vengeance. My heart slammed in my chest.

I just wanted it all to go away.

But I scooped up my purse and clothes and in a panic, ran into Nico's closet. Not the smartest place to hide, but closets seemed to be a pattern for me. I turned out the light and ran to the dresser I'd just been snooping through. Pushing it slightly away from the wall, I managed to squeeze behind it. If anyone entered the closet and looked really hard, they'd find me in seconds. But if they were rushing, I might be in luck.

I texted Nico.

intruders in the house. help me please

holy shit. i'll have colt & dom there in a minute. are you safe?

not sure. in your closet

heading home. be careful

Oh my god. I was going through this again. These people were ruthless, and I was beginning to realize there was no escaping them.

Would I spend the rest of my life looking over my shoulder?

CHAPTER 20

NICO

"WHAT THE FUCK IS GOING ON?" I demanded when I got home. I'd driven across Vegas at eighty miles per hour and was lucky I'd not killed myself or anyone else.

But there was one person I *did* intend to kill—the motherfucker who'd invaded my home.

You only pull that shit on me once. And you *don't* live to talk about it.

Colt and Dom directed my gaze toward the kitchen.

Had someone just punched me in the stomach?

There, in the middle of the floor lay Clare, my dutiful housekeeper, in a pool of blood with what appeared to be a vicious bullet wound to her chest.

She hadn't stood a chance. Why hadn't I realized how my work could put her life in danger? She'd probably been shot trying to protect the house and Rain.

But that's what I hired fucking security guards for. It's not the housekeeper's job to keep the goddamn place safe.

Heads were going to roll. An innocent life had just been wasted, and I was about to lose my shit.

I knelt by her side, avoiding the blood, and ran my hand over her still-warm forehead. Her eyes were open, staring at the kitchen ceiling.

Goddammit.

"There's more. Upstairs," Colt said.

My heart pounded until I had trouble breathing. I stroked Clare's cheek and silently thanked her. Then, I forced myself to move, and ran up the steps two at a time with Colt on my heels.

Had the intruder gotten to Rain?

Was my day about to get a lot fucking worse?

I couldn't stomach losing another woman I loved. One had been enough for my lifetime.

As I reached the top of the stairs, we found another lifeless body in a pool of blood that was rapidly soaking into the rug under it. I poked at it with the toe of my shoe, and a dead man rolled over, thin and lanky.

Who the hell was that?

"Where is Rain?" I growled.

Dom joined us at the top of the stairs and gestured with his head. "In your room."

Terrified of what I might find, I pushed the door open. My bed was unmade from the night before, and my clothes lay in the pile where I'd left them. But there was no sign of Rain.

Just as I turned to Dom and Colt to ask them what the hell was going on, a small whimper came from inside my closet.

"What the—"

I rushed inside and found Rain—my poor Rain—cowering in a corner in my too-big bathrobe, clutching her clothes and purse in a small bundle as if for protection. At the sound of my approaching steps, she winced. But when she saw it was me, a weak smile materialized on her face.

"Are you okay?" I asked in a panic, crouching to look her over for signs of injury.

"We got here just in time, Nico," Dom said from the closet doorway. "A moment longer, and I'm not sure what would have happened. She's unharmed, but we couldn't get her to come out."

I knew what would have happened. I never would have seen Rain again—at least not alive. And the thought of that sickened me to the core.

I pulled her to me, kissing the top of her head. I was one big ball of regret over not having protected her well enough.

I sure hadn't protected Clare, and now she was gone. What a fucking waste.

"Guys," I said, the words sticking in my throat, "I don't know how to thank you. Your fast work saved Rain."

I got to my feet and pulled Rain to hers then hugged each of the guys.

As much as I complained about them, they had my back like the champs that they were. I'd be nothing without my childhood friends.

Dom explained, "As you can see, we shot him down just as he arrived at your bedroom door. We think he threatened the housekeeper to reveal Rain's where-abouts, and when she didn't, he shot her."

Rain gasped when she learned Clare's fate.

The killer didn't seem to need Clare's help—he'd nearly found his target quite well on his own.

The fucker had taken her out for nothing.

"Rain, can you take a look at the guy in the hallway? The man is dead, and I know it won't be pleasant, but I want to know if he's the one from the restaurant yesterday."

She nodded. "Yeah. I can do it."

We walked her over to where he lay, and she gasped, nodding.

"It's him. It's him," she whispered. "How did he find us? How did he find me?" she asked with wide eyes.

I tightened my arm around her shaking body. "I don't know. But I'm going to find out. Let's get out of here."

I led her out the front of the house rather than through the kitchen so she wouldn't have to see Clare's body. After I'd helped her into the shower in her cottage, I stepped outside to see if Colt or Dom had anything to add that they'd not wanted to say in front of Rain.

"How the hell did he breach our security, goddammit?" I asked, although I was certain they were asking themselves the same question.

Colt shook his head. "Dunno. But I'll look into it. It could have been way worse than just taking off with Rain. Those guys would have killed any of us to get to her."

I glanced over at the guard shack, now on high alert and manned by two security personnel whose weapons were drawn and ready.

"Nico, there's something Colt and I wanted to talk to you about," Dom said carefully.

"Okay."

Colt looked down, shifting uncomfortably. "Look, we know you're trying to help Rain find her sister—"

"*We're* trying to help Rain find her sister," I corrected.

He nodded. "Yeah. Right. Well, we think that having her here, in the compound, is compromising everything we've worked for."

I frowned. "I don't get it. What are you saying?"

"It's too dangerous to have her here. She's putting us all in danger, Nico," Colt said.

"We, um, think your judgment might be a bit... clouded lately," Dom added. "You're not thinking clearly. You've gotten attached. We don't blame you. Rain's a beautiful woman. But it's not serving you well."

Whether he was right or wrong, fury flooded my veins. "Go fuck yourselves," I said, and returned to the cottage.

"Feeling better?" I asked when Rain emerged from the shower, towel drying her hair.

"Yeah. Thank you. And thanks to Dom and Colt, too." She shook her head. "These people, the traffickers, they're never going to leave me alone are they? I know this one guy is dead, but there are others. There will always be others, right?"

Not if I had my way.

CHAPTER 21

NICO

"GET DRESSED. We're going to do something fun," I told Rain.

She shrugged. "Okay. Give me a sec."

Thirty minutes later, Smitt drove us into the heliport, where a young woman approached us with a clipboard.

"Nico and Rain? Would you like to come this way?" she asked.

Rain clutched my hand when I took hers, and I couldn't help stealing a look at how her hair whipped around her face as we crossed the tarmac. I stopped to move a chunk of it aside so she could see, and she laughed.

"What are we doing here? Going for a plane ride?"

"Something like that."

We approached an Airbus AS350, and she stopped in her tracks. "We're going on a helicopter ride?"

I nodded, and she jumped up and down in delight. My plan to take her mind off all the shit swirling around just might work, if only temporarily.

The concierge opened the helicopter door, and we climbed in.

"Now this is a surprise," Rain said, grinning, a hint of sadness lingering behind her eyes.

The pilot had us buckle up and put our headphones on, and in minutes, we were airborne.

"Where are we going?" Rain asked, her voice metallic through the headphones.

"Grand Canyon."

Her eyes widened. "No way. Oh my god, I've always wanted to fly over the Grand Canyon."

Her forehead pressed against the window for the entire flight, and she continually nudged me to point out things of interest in between snapping photos with her phone.

I liked how someone from her background could get excited about a helicopter ride. I'd wondered if she was going to be jaded or spoiled, but she was proving me wrong. While she watched the scenery a thousand feet below, I watched *her*, gorgeous in faded jeans and a simple white shirt.

When we arrived at Grand Canyon West, the helicopter began to descend.

"What are we doing?" she asked with a frown.

I pointed. "We're landing in the canyon. We'll have a picnic lunch and some wine, and then fly out."

"Are you kidding? Oh my god!"

When we touched on the canyon floor, I grabbed our lunch cooler and blanket, and we stepped out onto the sandy ground. Carefully walking around rocks and brushy plants, we found a clearing and took a seat.

"This is incredible. We're the only ones here," Rain said.

"Except for that helicopter flying overhead and our pilot having a smoke over there."

She laughed. It was nice to see her relaxed, not preoccupied by, well, everything.

She sipped her wine and lay back on our blanket to stare at the cloudless blue sky. "So, I snooped a little in your room this morning. You know, before the hit man came over and turned your house into utter carnage."

"What? Why?"

She shrugged. "I don't really know. I was in your closet just looking around, and slid open the top drawer of your dresser. I saw her picture."

I nodded. It wasn't like I had anything to hide per se, but it was odd to have someone go through my things and then cop to it. And now she knew about one of the worst things to ever happen to me.

"Yeah. She left me. One day, she packed her bag and just said goodbye. It was like a death. I'd thought we'd be together forever."

But nothing was forever, I'd learned. What a naïve sap I'd been.

Rain propped her head up on one hand. "Geez. I'm sorry. That sounds terrible."

I looked up at the top of the canyon where a huge bird circled overhead, hunting for his next meal.

"I was selfish and neglectful. I'd like to think I've learned."

Christ, I *hoped* I'd learned.

"You know more about love, now?" she asked.

I had to laugh at that. "Not really."

She looked around at the stunning scenery and the sadness returned to her face. I knew it wasn't far from the surface. "My sister may never get to see anything like this." She made a sweeping gesture, and then drew her hand to cover her mouth.

I reached out and pulled her to me. "I'm telling you, Rain, we'll find her. One way or the other."

She looked relieved at my confidence.

I wished I felt the same way.

CHAPTER 22

RAIN

NOT ONLY DID I get to see the Grand Canyon from the air, but I also visited the bottom of it with the handsome Nico.

At least there was one thing going right in my life. Sort of.

What a freaking day.

Almost get murdered in the morning, fly to the Grand Canyon in the afternoon.

I was nothing short of traumatized by what had happened, and while I was moved that Nico took me on a day trip to take my mind off it, it was never far from my thoughts.

How could it be?

But I put on a brave face and was as engaging as I

could be, smiling, flirting, and trying generally to not be a buzz kill.

When we got back to the compound, Nico led me straight to his house, where I guessed my privileges were still intact. Maybe my days of being locked up in the cottage were over?

I was relaxed and a little buzzed from the wine and looked forward to curling up in front of the fireplace in his study to ward off the chill of the desert night. But my memory of the dead guy right outside his room was going to haunt me for a long, long time.

Amazingly, all signs of the struggles of the morning had vanished. If you hadn't known what had gone down, well, you'd have no freaking idea. The house was spotless.

I wondered who'd gotten the unenviable job of cleaning up two dead bodies and all the blood they'd left behind. I wasn't going to ask.

I was just glad it wasn't me.

"It's so terrible about Clare," I said. "Did she have any family?"

Nico shook his head. "No, at least none that I knew of. She lived in one of the cottages here on the property. It's awful. And all my fault."

I reached for his hand. "Don't blame yourself."

When we got to his study, I kissed the corner of his mouth. And when I did, he put his hands on either side of my face and pressed his lips to mine hungrily.

I wanted to forget the morning and feel good. I needed to feel good.

He began to unbutton my blouse and in seconds, it fell from my shoulders. He sat on the sofa and pulled me on top to straddle him.

He unhooked my white lace bra, and as I offered him my breasts, he pushed them together and buried his face.

"Touch yourself," he demanded.

I unzipped my jeans, and slipping my hand inside them, went straight for my hard clit and soaked folds. I pressed my lips to Nico's again and moved my hips over my fingers as he continued to play with my breasts.

"Fucking hot," he growled.

As I stroked myself, I put pressure on Nico's cock, hard and straining against his fly. I was dying to get my mouth on him, but I wanted to make our fun last.

"Um, excuse me," a male voice said from the doorway.

I shrieked and pulled my hand out of my pants, covering my tits. Who the hell was in the house, now?

Nico peered around me as I looked over my shoulder and found Dom standing there, *watching* us.

What the fuck?

Didn't he have his own house?

I'd never given the guy much thought. I guess I was always overwhelmed in Nico's presence, susceptible to his charms as I was. Although I was mortified at Dom's little intrusion, his wicked smile sent a shiver up my naked spine. I kept my hands covering my chest and my back turned but felt a strange urge to bare it all for him.

Was I an exhibitionist?

"Dom, what's up?" Nico asked patiently.

Why wasn't he pissed? Why wasn't he telling him to get the hell out?

Over my shoulder, I watched Dom walk into the room.

The nerve.

"I heard someone having a good time. Thought I'd check and see what was going on."

What? Nico sat back on the sofa, arms spread, smiling at me. Was this some sort of game they played?

If that's what they wanted, then game on.

I dropped my arms and turned to face Dom with my hands on my hips.

He just tilted his head, checking out my bare breasts and unbuttoned jeans.

"You're beautiful, Rain," he said quietly.

A vulnerable look crossed his face, and something tingled between my legs.

Easy girl.

"Dom, what are you doing, here?" I asked innocently.

He was checking me out. And I liked it.

I didn't like to admit it, but there it was.

Nico cleared his throat. "He likes to watch."

Seriously?

I probably should have told him to hit the road, but I was feeling pretty loose thanks to the wine and the general status of my life having turned into a freaky shit show.

"Watch? Watch what?" I asked.

Nico cleared his throat. "Dom, I think you'd better go. Not sure Rain's comfortable with your being here."

Dom sighed deeply, his gaze not breaking from mine. "Really, Rain? Do you want me to leave? Because I will." He started backing up.

Holy crap. Did they want to have a threesome? Did I want to have a threesome? I'd thought about it plenty of times, but never imagined it unfolding quite like this.

"No. Wait," I said, quickly, surprising the hell out of myself. "Don't go."

A slow smile crept across his face, and he took a couple steps toward me.

Oh my god. Why was this exciting me so much?

"You okay with this?" Nico asked.

Watching. That was Dom's kink. Interesting. But would he want more?

"I'm good, Nico. It's okay."

I pushed my jeans down over my hips, standing in front of both guys wearing only a lacy thong.

"Turn around," Dom ordered.

Holy crap. Take orders from *two* guys?

I stared him down for a moment, then turned to face Nico, who was gazing up at me with his own half-smile.

"C'mere," Nico said.

I walked up to him where he remained seated on the sofa. He hooked his thumbs in my thong and whipped it to the floor.

"Kneel," he said, placing a pillow at my feet.

I got down on it and heard Dom settle into a crackly leather chair somewhere behind me.

"Now, open my pants."

I leaned forward and released Nico's raging hard-on. Without waiting for any direction, I bent to lick the precum off his tip. Something about knowing Dom was behind me made me ravenous for Nico.

Shit. Two beautiful men and there I was, naked as the day I was born.

"Suck me, Rain."

Well, he didn't have to ask twice.

I rubbed my lips over his head until he sucked in his breath, fully aware that my position afforded his friend a clear view of my pussy and ass.

And I loved it. I couldn't believe it, but I loved it.

I ran my lips all the way down Nico's cock to the root and back up again, imagining Dom's eyes on me.

"Fuck, baby, feels so good."

I pulled him out of my mouth. "Yeah? You like it?"

He smiled down on me, and god, he was beautiful.

"I like it and Dom likes it," he said, gesturing behind me.

I took a quick look over my shoulder. Dom sat, hands resting on the chair's arms, looking quite content. He nodded when I looked at him.

Wow. Watching really *was* his thing.

And I loved it.

"C'mon, babe. Climb on top," Nico said, reaching into a pocket and retrieving a condom.

Once he'd covered himself, I straddled his lap again.

"Open your pussy for me."

With one hand on the sofa back, I spread my lips so Nico could see my most private parts. Holding his cock, he directed it to my opening and with his free hand, pulled me down on top of him.

I arched my back to give Dom a better view.

I screamed from the initial fullness, which in moments gave way to a pulsing that radiated from my core to the ends of my limbs. With Nico's hands on my hips, I clasped the back of his neck and we rode each other in perfect rhythm. He watched me buck my head as my first orgasm hit me like a speeding truck, and he held me tight to still my trembling.

How did this man make me feel so safe when everything around me screamed I should run far away and hide? And how did we connect at such an intense physical level when we'd barely just met?

I didn't understand it at all. But that was okay.

A small growl built in Nico's chest, and he dropped his head back, eyes squeezed shut. In moments, it turned into a holler as he pistoned me up and down while he came.

As he caught his breath, I wiped the sweat from his temples, and glanced back over my shoulder.

Dom was gone.

CHAPTER 23

RAIN

I woke to the sounds of Nico getting dressed. It was still dark.

"What's going on? What time is it?" I asked, yawning.

He came over and kissed the top of my head, his care washing over me. How the hell did he do that?

"Go back to sleep. I have to go to work for a while. Leo called me. Something's up, I think with his dad."

Leo's dad? This was a story I'd need to hear later.

He paused at the bedroom door and looked back like he wanted to say something. But he just left, pulling the door closed.

Who went to work in the middle of the night?

People like Nico, Dom, and Colt did, that was who.

I was surrounded by some crazy shit, in a freaking

compound, watched by guards with guns, where people occasionally got shot.

I'd come to Vegas for a fun weekend. And now I couldn't get out. People were after me, and my beautiful sister was gone. It was like I'd landed in hell.

And I was fucking some hot mobster and letting his pervy friend watch.

Jesusfuckingchrist.

I was tempted to get up and do something. Anything.

But there was nothing I *could* do. At least at the moment.

I closed my eyes for some more sleep, hoping to hell I wouldn't have nightmares.

And just as I was dozing off, the bedroom door opened. "Hey, you're back already."

But Nico didn't say anything.

"Nico, get in bed will you, I'm cold." I shivered under the sheets.

Still nothing.

So I turned over to see that in the dark, I could just make out his silhouette against the bedroom door.

Why was he just standing there?

"Nico? You okay?" I asked.

Just then my phone buzzed with a new text.

still working. be home later, sleeping beauty

It was from Nico.

So who the fuck was in my bedroom?

I fumbled for the light on the nightstand. "Who are you? Get the hell out!"

But by the time I got the light on, whoever it was, was gone.

The terror of the day before came rushing back like a merciless tidal wave, engulfing me and sucking me in. Was there no escape from my fear?

Trembling, I pushed myself out of the bed and stumbled to lock the bedroom door. A lot of good that would do, but for a moment I felt a modicum safer.

It must have been Dom, that weirdo. I'd not only have Nico deal with him later, but next time I saw him, I'd give him a piece of my mind, too. It was one thing to watch when he had my consent. But in the middle of the night, he certainly did not.

Asshole.

"Fuck you, Dom," I screamed through the door. As if he could hear me. He was probably back in his own place by now, jerking off.

Ugh. Why had I let him watch? I was such an idiot.

I dragged a heavy upholstered chair across the room and set it in front of the door. It was a lame attempt at security, but it felt good, nevertheless.

I was tempted to text Nico and tell him, but I knew he'd rush home. I felt safe now, at least for the time being.

I knew I'd never get back to sleep, so I grabbed my phone and started reading a sweet romance novel, hoping it would take me someplace happy.

"Hi, Mom," I said as cheerfully as I could on my cell phone.

I looked around Nico's kitchen, where I'd helped myself to a bowl of cereal.

Where Clare had been murdered just the day before. I couldn't believe I was sitting where she once had, cooking meals for Nico with all the passion of someone who takes great pride in their work. Sadness washed through me.

But I couldn't succumb to despair just yet. I had my mother to deal with. And I wanted to forget all about Dom.

"Hi honey. Put Mazzy on the line. I haven't talked to her in ages."

Shit. I'd known this moment was coming. Of course, she was going to wonder why I was the one always checking in.

"Oh, Mom, she just ran down to the hotel shop to get some water."

Yeah, right.

"Huh. Well, I called her on her cell the other day, and she didn't pick up."

"She's having the best time, Mom. I'll have her call you. You know how she gets absorbed in things and just forgets everything else in the world. I don't even know if she's charged her phone since she's been here."

God, I wanted to die over the lies I was telling my

mother. It wasn't right on so many levels. But if what Nico said was true, alerting her could make it less likely we'd see Mazzy safely returned.

And that had to be my top priority. At least at the moment.

I signed off with Mom.

Another day, another raft of lies.

CHAPTER 24

NICO

"HEY, ASSHOLE," I snarled, barging into Dom's office.

He looked up from his computer. "Nico. How's it going? Hey, that was pretty hot with Rain—"

"What were you doing in my room this morning?"

Confusion crossed his face. He'd always been good at playing dumb. When we were kids, the bastard could get out of any scrape. It had always amazed me.

And now it was pissing me off.

He frowned. "What the hell are you talking about? What's wrong with you?"

"Did you or did you not enter my bedroom this morning when Rain was in there alone?"

He recoiled. "Of course not. Are you fucking crazy? What are you talking about?"

So help me, if he were lying...

"Are you saying you did *not* enter my room this morning when I was out, and stand in the doorway, scaring the shit out of Rain?"

He looked at me like I was insane.

I sort of was, at least at that moment.

Why was I losing my shit over her? It wasn't like she was my girlfriend. Yeah, we'd had some kick-ass sexy fun, and she was beyond stunning, but she'd go back home to LA first chance she got.

And that would be the end of that.

Dom walked around his desk to face me. "I couldn't have been in your room this morning, or any time after I left you guys. I went to see that girl we know, the one who works at the strip club. I spent the night with her and just got back an hour or so."

I stared, wanting to believe him.

I'd let him watch before, but I was beginning to regret it, even though Rain hadn't seemed to mind. On the contrary, I think she'd come harder than I ever seen her.

He stood and walked around to the front of his desk. "Could it have been Colt?" he asked.

I looked down, pacing the floor. "I don't see how. He's out of town. At least I think he is."

"Was it another trafficker? Those fuckers don't give up."

I'd had enough. No more taking chances. "I'm gonna assign Smitt to stay with her 24/7. I think that's the only way to keep her safe."

If it wasn't Dom, who the fuck had it been? The top-notch security we paid a lot of money for was being breached left and right. It was time for drastic measures.

I found Rain in her cottage, sitting in silence, wrapped in a blanket, sipping tea on her sofa.

"Hey sweetie," I said, kissing her temple.

"Hey," she said quietly.

"It wasn't Dom."

Her gaze snapped in my direction. "Huh?"

"He was out all night with a girl he sees. Got home an hour ago."

She shook her head. "Someone was there. I know it. I've asked myself if I were imagining it, but I'm sure I wasn't. Could it have been Colt?"

I shook my head. "Doesn't sound like the sort of thing he'd do, plus I'm pretty sure he's out of town anyway."

She took my hand, her own still warm from her coffee cup. "I really miss my parents."

Funny she'd mentioned her parents.

"I've been thinking…" I started. "They need to know what's happened to your sister. But we can only tell them if they promise not to bring in the authorities. At least not yet."

She whipped around toward me. "Oh yes! I think we should tell them. I just cannot lie any longer."

That afternoon we were on our way to the airport for another helicopter ride, this time to LA. I wanted to be there when Rain told her parents about Mazzy, if for no other reason than to support her and make sure they understood that should they alert the authorities, it would lesson the likelihood they'd ever see their daughter again.

"They're never going to forgive me. Not that I blame them."

She was probably right, and I was partly at fault for that, since I'd insisted so hard that she *not* inform them.

But I couldn't ask Rain to suffer alone any longer, keeping all that had happened a secret from her parents with continual lies and deceptions.

"They've got to be suspicious that something is up. How many people hang out in Vegas for longer than a week? There are only so many spa days you can do and shows you can see. How do you manage living here?"

I looked out the window of the taxi taking us to her parents' house. "I have Dom and Colt and my business dealings with Leo and Luca. It's a nice break after the craziness of New York. Yeah, sometimes it's a little strange after having been on the East Coast for so long, but I kind of like the wide-open space."

I yawned, having been up most of the night. Speaking of Leo and Luca, someone had come forward with information about their dad.

Well, he hadn't exactly *voluntarily* come forward. When I'd arrived at Leo's office in the middle of the night, the informer was sitting in a chair surrounded by three guns pointed at his head.

Turned out that when Luca and Leo took out their mother's murderer, Sal, the old man's entire operation began to fall apart. One particularly bold fucker actually went as far as to try and bribe the twins for information about their dad. That guy had just significantly decreased the likelihood that he'd live to be an old man.

Turned out Sal had known where their father was all those years. He'd driven him out of town by threatening to murder his family.

I guess that would make a father split.

The only question now was whether Mr. Borroni was still alive.

And we were going to find out one way or the other.

CHAPTER 25

NICO

OUR CAB PULLED up to Rain's parents' home, a sprawling Beverly Hills mansion exactly as I'd pictured it, tastefully landscaped and unobtrusive aside from its massiveness.

"Oh god. I'm so nervous," she said, wiping her hands on her skirt.

She turned to me just before we got out of the cab. "I'm telling them you and I are dating, okay? That should answer some of the questions they'll have."

I was sure they'd have a lot of questions when Rain walked into the house with a man they'd not only never met, but had never even heard of.

But I knew we'd done the right thing the way Rain's face brightened when the front door was opened by the housekeeper.

"Oh my god, I'm so happy to see you," she said, throwing her arms around the woman's neck.

"Miss Rain, how are you? Are you and Miss Mazzy home, now?" she asked when she finally let her go. She looked me up and down in confusion, and then behind us like she expected Mazzy to come right up the front walk.

Rain brushed away the tears in her eyes, and nodded. "I'm fine Sylvia, just happy to be home. And not, I'm not staying. But I will be home for good, soon. Mazzy too."

She glanced at me.

"Okay, Miss Rain. Follow me, your parents are having drinks before dinner."

The house was what I expected of an LA mansion, with soaring ceilings, marble floors, and a sweeping center hall staircase. There were huge oil paintings all over, many of which I assumed were done by Rain.

Christ, she'd grown up with this opulence. I lived very well now, but I couldn't imagine having had her sort of wealth all my life.

"Nico, these are my parents, Mark and Susie Spector."

A good-looking couple stood to greet me.

Rain clearly took after her mother, an elegant middle-aged woman in slim jeans and a linen blouse. Her father, almost my height, was fit and healthy with thick salt and pepper hair and a friendly smile.

"How do you do?" I said, shaking their hands.

"Welcome to our home, Nico," Mark said. "Would you like a scotch?"

Christ, I'd like five scotches. But I kept that to myself.

"Have a seat over here with me, why don't you," Rain's father said after handing me a rocks glass filled to the brim.

I liked him already.

I settled into a crackly leather chair, much like the ones I had in my own study.

Mark leaned forward on his knees, while Rain and her mom huddled together on the other side of the room over glasses of white wine.

"How'd you and Rain meet?"

"At the Venetian Hotel. I was there meeting a friend for a drink, and we all got into the same elevator," I semi-lied.

He nodded, clearly checking me out.

I would have done the same with a man my daughter had brought home.

But I was saved by the housekeeper, who called us to the dining room for dinner.

"Rain, your paintings are amazing," I said as we settled into the table.

She blushed a little, which got my motor revving.

Down boy—we were at her goddamned parents' house.

"Thanks," she said shyly. "It's kind of embarrassing that they are plastered *all over* the place, but I do appreciate my parents' support." She reached toward her mother and squeezed her hand.

It was something to see Rain in her element. She was a lucky girl. Her parents adored her. Now if only I could get their second daughter back...

"We wouldn't hang them if they weren't exceptional works of art, honey. I've told you that," Mark said.

"Thanks, Dad."

We had just begun our meal of a delicious roast chicken when Rain's mother started asking the inevitable questions.

"You know, Rain, it's so funny that your sister didn't want to come with you. And how long are you staying in Vegas, anyway?"

Rain glanced my way, her eyes full of panic. But she knew what to do. We'd discussed it on the way there.

She set down her fork, and her mom, sensing something was wrong, did the same.

Amazing how people could be so connected.

"Mom, Dad, the reason I've stayed on in Vegas hasn't been to go to spas or shows."

Now her dad put down his fork, too.

"Mazzy is missing, and Nico is helping me look for her."

Mark slammed his hand on the dining table, sending two wine glasses flying. He didn't even notice.

"Are you goddamn kidding me? Something happened to your sister, and you didn't tell us?"

Susie covered her mouth, but a sob escaped anyway.

Rain's lower lip began to tremble. "I know. I know. I wanted to tell you but I knew you'd call the cops—"

"Of course we'd call the cops, Rain!" her father shouted.

"Dad, listen, please."

Her mom jumped up, wringing her hands, and began pacing. "Mark, call the family lawyer. He'll get a private investigator looking," she said, her voice breaking.

"*Mom*, listen to me," Rain said in a raised voice.

That caught the attention of both her parents.

"We are pretty sure she was taken by traffickers—"

Susie froze. "What? What did you just say?"

Rain look from her dad to her mom, and back, tears streaming down her face. "It's true, Mom. It's true. Traffickers got our Mazzy."

At that, Susie fell to her knees. "No, no, no. My baby!" she wailed.

Rain ran to her and took her by the shoulders. "Mom, Nico knows people in Vegas, and he and his business partners can get information the cops can't."

Mark, now standing, lunged in my direction. "Is this true, Nico? Because if it is, I want you to get your ass back out there and get looking for her *right now*," he shouted, slamming his hand on the table again.

I held my hands up, hoping to calm the situation, but knowing it was probably impossible. I'd be losing my shit if my daughter were missing, too.

"Sir, one of my business partners has a connection

to the trafficking ring that operates in Las Vegas. He's getting information about your daughter, as we speak."

I looked over at Rain, clinging to her mother, her shoulders shaking with sobs. "I'm sorry, I'm so sorry," she kept mumbling.

Her dad put his hands on the back of his dining chair, and for a moment, I wondered if he was going to pick it up and break it over something.

Like my head.

"What do you mean, you have *connections*? Are you involved in some sort of underworld yourself?" he demanded.

I'd known this question was coming.

"I invest in casinos, and am part-owner in some retail properties in Las Vegas. That's all I can really tell you," I said.

Her dad looked confused then pissed. "I don't know what the hell kind of answer that is, and I'm not sure I want to know. Young man, I will give you forty-eight hours to come up with information about my daughter. After that, I am notifying the authorities, as well as my own legal team."

The screws were tightening.

"Fair enough," I said.

He looked at Rain. "And you are going nowhere. You'll stay here with your mother and me."

But Rain shook her head. "I can't, Dad. Apparently, they're after me, too. For the time being, Nico can keep me safer than anyone."

Her father looked like he was going to explode, while Rain pulled her mother up off the floor. The housekeeper stood in a corner, crying as well.

"I can assure you, Mr. Spector, that I will not only take care of Rain, but also find your Mazzy. You have my word."

If only I were as convinced.

CHAPTER 26

RAIN

ON THE HELICOPTER ride back to Vegas, Nico and I didn't say a word to each other. I hated to leave my parents so destroyed and I hated myself for all the lies I'd told them.

My dad had come down hard on him—but I'd seen that coming. He was a successful businessman and was not used to someone else calling the shots. The whole thing was torturous for him, letting a man he barely knew take over the search for his youngest daughter.

It wasn't much easier for my mom and me. We'd left her in tears, a crumpled mess on the living room sofa. She'd not touched a bite of her dinner, and I knew she wouldn't be able to eat again until Mazzy came home.

They'd been good parents, if a little overprotective at times, and didn't deserve this. My dad had always hoped I'd follow him into his business, and when it became clear I was heading for a career in the arts, Mazzy was his last hope. They had a special bond since she'd worked summers for him as a teenager.

My parents might have been rich, but they'd never spoiled us. We'd always worked for the privileges we were granted.

It couldn't have been easy for Nico, either. He was an alpha male, just like my dad, and he was not used to having to answer to someone. But he deferred to my dad, and I appreciated the respect he'd shown him.

I wouldn't have it any other way. Whether he and I were a couple or not, he saw how I respected my parents and was smart enough to follow my lead.

I was comforted knowing that the two men had reached an agreement on a path forward, and I was confident Nico could make something happen in the forty-eight hours my dad had given him. The last thing I wanted to see was my dad start up a search for Mazzy. That could kill my parents, learning about the horrible world their youngest daughter had been dragged into.

Sometimes it was best if parents didn't know everything.

And if Mazzy didn't come home? I couldn't even think about that. It would certainly be the end of my parents as I knew them.

As Smitt drove us back to the estate, I shuddered in spite of the warm car.

Nico finally spoke. "Wish I could have met your parents under better circumstances. They seem like nice people."

I nodded. I'd thought of that, too. If Nico had met them as just the guy I was dating rather than a Vegas businessman with ties to the city's underground, what would that have been like?

But dating Nico? In what world would that happen other than the strange one I'd recently been thrust into?

And what were we now, anyway? Two people looking for comfort, who knew they'd go their separate ways sooner rather than later?

"They are nice people. Sorry my dad shouted so much, although I guess I can't blame him. I hated leaving them there, so devastated." I started getting choked up again.

So tired of crying.

"I'm glad we told them. It was the right thing to do. But seeing them suffer... I don't know what's worse than that. They don't deserve it. I should have stayed home with them."

"It's to be expected, that sort of reaction. I've seen it before," he said.

He didn't elaborate, and I wasn't sure I wanted him to.

"But you know you can't stay at their house. We need to keep you safe for the time being. You wouldn't have done your parents a lot of good if you were captured, too, and their lives endangered."

I leaned my head against the car window, overcome with a sudden exhaustion. Guess coming clean with your parents will take a lot out of you. "I think I'd like to sleep in the cottage tonight."

He shook his head. "We can't risk that. I want you in my room where I can see you. Smitt will be in the next room over, in case anything happens. I've briefed all the guards, as well as Dom, and Colt is back in town. Everyone's on alert. If you want time to yourself, I'll sleep in the study. But we're keeping the door between the two rooms open. You can paint in the cottage but at night you'll be in the house."

Wow. Nico's set-up was like freaking Fort Knox.

And if it was like Fort Knox, why didn't I feel safer?

be ready to go out at six tonight

Well, then. If Nico wanted me ready to go out, then ready I would be.

A bit of light pushed across my black mood, which had been only marginally helped by spending the day painting. Of course, Smitt and another armed guard were stationed right outside my door, pacing back and forth with their giant weapons, occasionally speaking on the microphones clipped to the front of their bullet-proof vests.

I was living in a combat zone.

I finally turned my easel away from the window so I wouldn't be so distracted by the guys pacing out front, but it was Nico's invitation to—where were we going? —that gave me something to look forward to.

From my closet, I pulled out a silky acid-yellow jumpsuit that had come from Nico's boutique. I'd normally never wear something so flashy, but what the hell—it was Vegas, the place where people climbed out of their normal lives to be someone different for just a while.

I looked at it as a sort of costume. And I was a different person.

Just for a few hours, I wanted no worries. No thinking about my parents at home, dying for information about my sister, no terrible visions of what Mazzy might be going through, and no memory of my own close-call abduction.

I'd be just a girl out for a night of fun with a devastatingly gorgeous man, dressed to the nines, having a great time.

Yeah, right.

How many times had I wished I could go back to the last night I saw Mazzy? So many things that I could have done differently, starting with not letting her run off with a stranger. What had she been thinking?

What had *I* been thinking?

She'd been mesmerized by the fantasy land that was Vegas. Back at home, Mazzy never would have hooked up with a stranger, and if she'd even tried, I would not have let her.

So how did we fuck up so badly? We *knew* better.

I blew my hair out with a lot of spray for a bouncy, movie-star look since I was aiming for all-out glamour, and painted on a serious smoky eye.

"Damn. Look at you," Nico said when he showed up at the cottage door.

I shrugged. "I'm trying to be someone different for a few hours. Someone with no problems."

"I don't blame you. Let's go."

The Vegas sunset was stunning that night, streaks of pink smeared across the sky like the universe was trying to make up for some of the shitty things it did every day.

I imagined it like a peace offering.

"Don't hate me. I can do good things, too," it seemed to say.

Smitt pulled up in front of a gallery in the newly developed artsy part of town. I knew the area from their Open Studio nights, where you could visit different artists and see what they were working on.

I hoped that I would someday, have a studio where I'd be proud to have visitors. But it was too soon for that. I still had a long way to go before my paintings were ready for prime time.

Nico opened my door and reached for my hand. God, his manners made me want to melt.

What a contradiction—someone immersed in his

world, who was also such an elegant gentleman. Well, except when he was killing someone.

"I've never been to this particular gallery," I said, as we passed by some reporters shouting questions and taking pictures of everyone as they went in. "Is someone important exhibiting?"

He nodded and smiled. "Yes, several important people are."

I had to give him credit. He knew what I liked, and was trying to preoccupy me with it.

He got me.

Did I just say that? Cheesy.

A waitress floated by with a tray of champagne flutes. Nico and I each grabbed one, but I'd been tempted to take two. I knew the first glass was going to go down fast.

Very fast.

"You look fucking amazing, baby," Nico murmured in my ear, as he discreetly passed a hand over the silk clinging to my ass cheeks.

I knew he'd be happy.

"You don't look too badly your—"

But I couldn't finish my sentence.

My stomach dropped, and a wave of humiliation reddened my face.

"What the fuck is that?"

CHAPTER 27

RAIN

NICO TURNED to the gallery wall where I was pointing, smiled, then turned back to me.

"That, my dear, is one of your paintings," he said.

"What is it doing *here*?" I demanded.

He took my hand and led me to a corner, which he backed me into. He moved closer, until I was trapped. Under any other circumstances, I would have been turned on. But at that moment I was confused. And my confusion was quickly giving way to anger.

"You are a talented painter. But you don't see it," he said quietly. "You never would have shown any of your work without your hand being forced."

"That is total bullshit—" I started to say.

"Stop." He pressed a finger against my lips. "Look at

the people clustered around it. It's getting more attention than any other painting here."

I peered behind him, wishing I'd worn something more subdued so I could meld into the background. Several people were looking at it, chattering among themselves.

Were they admiring it? Or talking about what a disaster it was?

"They love it. Look at the expressions on their faces."

I pushed past Nico, toward my abstract painting of Mazzy. It was dark and disturbed, as a way to express the terrible time I imagined her going through. Painting it had been deeply personal, which is why I was pissed at Nico... but the crowd's reaction was interesting. As I moved closer, I was able to eavesdrop since they had no idea who I was.

"Sad, but also triumphant."

"I don't know. The woman looks imprisoned."

"To me, she looks free."

"Whose work is this? I'd like to see more."

I turned back to Nico, who'd remained in the corner where I'd left him. He leaned against the wall with his arms crossed, staring me down with those damn dark eyes of his.

How had his wife ever left him?

"Lovely, isn't it?"

I hadn't realized Colt had walked up on my right side.

"I wonder if it's for sale," he said, his head tilted while he studied it.

"No, it's not," I said too quickly.

His gaze snapped in my direction. "No?"

"Um, no, that's what I heard, anyway," I sputtered.

He looked a little crestfallen and ran his hand over his bald head. "Too bad." He turned to me. "Hey, don't you paint?"

I nodded and took a swig of my champagne.

Why did this man make me so nervous? I'd barely ever had a conversation with him.

"Yeah, a little," I lied to ward off any further questions.

I peeked over my shoulder and saw Nico chatting with the gallery owner.

Colt shook his head at me. "*You* painted this, didn't you?"

Heat passed over my face as I blushed several shades of pink. I hated that about myself, being so transparent. I nodded. "I don't want anyone to know. I didn't give Nico permission to exhibit it here."

"Well, modesty never got anyone anywhere. In fact, I'd like to introduce you to a collector who's very interested."

Oh fuck. I was not in the frame of mind to talk about my painting, especially when I was dressed like such a party girl.

"Come with me, Rain. I know they'd love to meet you." He gestured for me to follow.

Cripes. Nico was still engaged with the owner.

"Francesca, Jorge, I want you to meet Rain. She's responsible for the work of art you were so dearly coveting."

Ugh. Why did he have to put it like that? But I smiled.

Francesca, a small dark-haired beauty, extended her hand. "You're a true talent."

"So nice to meet you," Jorge said with a bow of his head in heavily accented English. "I'd like to talk to you about a show. A show of your work only. Nobody else's."

"Oh, I don't know if I'm ready—"

Jorge reached into his pocket and pulled out a cigarette and lighter. "Why don't you step outside with me? We'll chat while I take care of the disgusting habit I acquired growing up in Spain."

"Oh, I love Spain—"

Colt patted me on the back. "I'll leave you two to it, then." He smiled and disappeared into the crowd.

"Let's go," Jorge said.

I glanced back into the gallery but didn't see Nico anywhere.

"I'm not sure…"

One thing I *was* sure of was Nico wanting me to stay close by.

But Francesca had hold of one of my arms, and Jorge the other.

They tightened their grips.

"What are you guys doing?" I asked nervously. "Let me go."

I started twisting out of their hold, but we were already outside. Jorge's cigarette and lighter dropped to the sidewalk, and a black SUV screeched up in front.

"Get off me," I tried to scream, but Francesca's hand was pressed over my mouth.

The car door opened in front of me, and Jorge shoved me in.

CHAPTER 28

NICO

"THANKS again for squeezing in Rain's painting."

The gallery owner, Henry, rolled his eyes and laughed. "Tell me she wasn't pissed at you. No one wants their work shown before they're absolutely ready."

He was right.

"She was pretty displeased at first, but when she saw people checking it out, it was like a light bulb went off."

Sometimes you just needed a little push to believe you could ride a bike.

Henry nodded. "Good. Glad to hear it. I've only seen that one painting of hers, but it was really something. I'd like to see more and find out if having her own gallery show might be something we could discuss. Speaking of which, where is the lovely lady?"

We scanned the well-dressed crowd. It had been a fruitful night for Henry—there were *sold* stickers on the walls next to several of the paintings he'd shown that night, including the most expensive ones. Both he and the artists he represented were likely very happy.

In fact, someone had wanted to buy Rain's painting.

"I don't see her, Nico," Henry said.

Where the hell was she? All night long she'd stood out in the crowd like a lighthouse beacon with that yellow outfit.

A beautiful lighthouse beacon.

But now, she was nowhere to be seen.

"Thanks again, Henry," I said, shaking his hand. "I'm going to find Rain and head home. I'm exhausted."

I beelined for Dom and Colt who were kicking back with some of Henry's expensive scotch.

"Guys. Where is Rain?"

Dom jumped to his feet while Colt followed more slowly.

"What do you mean, Nico? She was just here," Dom said, looking around.

The evening's crowd had begun to thin, and it should have been easy to spot Rain.

Unless she was no longer in the gallery.

"Jesus," I mumbled, rubbing my chin.

I ran over to the ladies' room and barged in. It was empty.

As was the men's room when I checked there, too.

I was trying to keep my shit together, and while I was sure Rain was somewhere on the premises, the fear of her being gone reminded me of when my wife split. She might have left on her own accord, but it was still a loss of devastating proportion.

"Nico," Colt called, beckoning me across the room.

Dom stood with his hands on his hips, looking down at his shoes and shaking his head.

What the hell was going on?

"Um, Nico, I introduced her to a couple people who wanted to do a gallery show with her. She stepped outside with them, I think to have a smoke."

Jesus Christ. I was going to break his goddamn neck.

"First, Rain doesn't smoke. And second, you watched her leave the gallery? *Are you fucking kidding me, Colt?*"

Heads turned in our direction as my voice got louder. And I did not give a damn.

Colt rolled his eyes. "Nico, would you relax? Let's go look out front. I'm sure we'll find her there. She's probably lined up a gallery show that will make her rich and famous."

"Colt, you're a dumb fuck if you really did let her leave. What the hell is wrong with you?" Dom asked.

Colt stopped in his tracks. "Back off, asshole."

I pushed past both of them and ran outside.

No sign of Rain. Anywhere.

I dialed Leo and Luca to alert them.

"Hey. Rain is missing. I think she may have been taken from the gallery."

Leo agreed to get our security guys looking for her in the usual places—casinos, airports, bus stations, etc.

"You," I said, pushing Colt against the building's brick façade. "You fucking asshole. You let her slip right out the door. You're useless. No, worse than useless. If anything happens to her..."

I wanted to punch the smug look right off his face as he stood there looking at me. He didn't give a damn.

I turned away before I tore his fucking head off. "Dom, let's go. And, Colt, start calling your fucking friends. And *find* her."

We headed straight for the car, leaving Colt standing there like the loser he was.

I'd had my share of ups and downs. I'd triumphed over enemies to protect my family business. I'd taken out the Russians who'd messed with my card club in New York. I'd also been steamrolled by someone I'd loved.

It was why I'd left New York for Vegas. Too many memories. Time for a fresh start.

But I'd never been as angered as I was at that moment. Whoever had taken Rain was going to pay. Dearly.

Dom pulled into Vegas traffic. "Give me her coordinates, Nico."

I'd installed a tracker in Rain's phone at Dom's

urging. He'd been right to insist we do that, because it was about to save her life.

"Shit. It's not picking up her phone."

Dom gunned it through a yellow light. "Try it again."

"I did. Fuck. Do you think they did something with her phone?"

He smacked his hands on the steering wheel.

"Keep trying. Sometimes the satellite doesn't pick up the signal right away."

Bingo.

"Looks like they're traveling north," I said.

Dom whipped a U-turn in the middle of the road and sped up.

"I'm gonna fucking kill Colt," I murmured.

"Seriously. I don't know what he was thinking. But, Nico, she'll be fine. We'll get her back. I know we will."

I buried my throbbing head in my hands and inhaled deeply to calm my spiking pulse.

"Fuck!" I growled, punching the dashboard. "I met her parents just yesterday. Her dad wanted her to stay home in LA, but I insisted she come back to Vegas because she'd be safer with me."

Dom veered right and we were on the freeway. "How long have you felt this way about her?"

"Huh?"

He glanced at me. "How long? You know, Nico, how long?"

I knew exactly what he was asking.

I just didn't want to answer it.

But it was a good question. When had it started?

Had it been when I'd seen how concerned she was about her parents?

The first time she'd spent the night with me?

When I'd watched her paint from my bedroom window?

The way she'd tried to escape to help her sister and I'd found her hiding in the hotel closet?

Or when she'd chased me through the bowels of the Venetian to get her purse back?

Maybe it had been the first time I'd laid eyes on her that night in the elevator. When she'd been barefoot, high heels dangling from her wrist, looking pissed off at the world for reasons I'd find out about later?

"Pretty much the first time I saw her," I admitted.

"Yeah. I haven't seen you like this since..." His words tapered off.

We both knew who he was talking about.

The GPS showed we were getting closer to Rain's phone. If all was going according to plan, that meant we were getting closer to Rain, as well.

"Yeah. I haven't felt like this since Bex."

He nodded. "I'm happy for you, man. I always hoped you'd find a way out of the hell she left you in."

I wasn't so sure I was finding a way out of my hell, as I was finding a new way back in. If anything happened to Rain... well, I didn't know. Didn't want to think about it.

One thing was for certain, though. Her father would kill me, if not with his own hands, then using his power, influence, and money. Men like him got what they wanted in spades.

Just like I usually did.

"Nico, why do you suppose Colt let her go? I don't get it," Dom said.

I didn't get it, either. It didn't add up.

But I was going to find out.

CHAPTER 29

RAIN

IT HAD FINALLY HAPPENED.

The traffickers had gotten me. I suppose I'd known all along that they would. The bastards were just too persistent and wily. If Nico had locked me in a secret underground cell in some distant land and thrown away the key, they still would have found me. And taken me like they did my sister.

My parents. It was going to be so hard on them. Thank god I'd seen them just a couple days before. Nico would have to explain what had happened. My dad would probably punch out his lights, and Nico, out of respect, would not hit back.

That was one of the things I liked about him. He may have been an underground kind of guy, but he had respect when it was needed.

Hopefully my father wouldn't kill him. But then, I wasn't going to be around, so that wouldn't be my problem.

I had better things to worry about.

And now that I was being dragged down into the ugly underbelly of the criminal world, would I find Mazzy? Would we be able to suffer through our new lives together? Or would we be spirited off to opposite ends of the earth to live out the rest of our days as prisoners, each wondering how the other was?

A crush of sadness pushed me beyond tears, and I settled into a strange resignation. If my sister hadn't gone before me, and I didn't believe there was a chance of seeing her, would I be fighting harder to get away? Would I be angrier?

Maybe I deserved the same fate, since I'd let it happen to her.

My face was pressed into the backseat of the car I'd been shoved into so hard that I could barely breathe. But I didn't have it in me to protest—in fact, I hoped I'd be smothered. It might have been a terrible cop-out, but it would more or less take care of all the problems I was facing.

We swerved around a corner, and my abductor Jorge leaned harder on my head, uninterested in my comfort or even my ability to breathe. He'd handcuffed my arms behind my back the moment I was in the car, so there was pretty much not a damn thing I could do. Francesca had split the moment they'd shut the car door. Wonder how much she got paid for her part.

The driver sped up, just as something slammed against the car. Great. If I didn't die from my abduction, a car wreck would get me.

How was that for irony?

"What the fuck was that?" Jorge yelled. "Faster. Speed it up, goddammit!"

A phone buzzed, and he cleared his throat. "Hello. Yeah. Yeah, I've got her. Fuck, I don't know. Someone just slammed into our car. It must be them. Yes, I'm ready."

Maybe Nico was... no, it was too much to hope.

The car swerved again, and without purchase, I slid halfway off the seat onto the floor where something wet soaked right through my jumpsuit pant legs. I was twisted into the most uncomfortable position possible, as Jorge kept my head on the seat by leaning on it with his one free arm.

God, please let me die now.

"Hey," Jorge shouted. "Careful. They're coming up on the left!"

The driver grunted as he was clearly trying to control the car at top speed. "Tony, I don't think I can—"

Who was Tony?

A gunshot rang out. The car veered sharply to the right, throwing Jorge off me, leaving me crumpled on the car floor where I was wedged between the front and back, probably more protected than when I'd been on the actual seat.

"Shit!" Jorge yelled. "Don! Don, are you okay?" he screamed.

The car spun and slammed into several things I could not identify because I couldn't see a damn thing. Jorge was tossed from one side of the backseat to the other, but because I was wedged onto the floor, I only banged against the cushioned upholstery. It was hardly pleasant, but if I'd been properly on the back seat, it could have been far worse.

Small mercies.

The car stopped moving, having settled against god knew what, and Jorge squeezed my upper arm in a death grip that I knew would leave a bruise.

Like that was the biggest of my concerns.

"C'mon. Move it," he growled.

I was yanked up onto the backseat, and that's when I realized Jorge had a gun in his hand. He looked around maniacally, his dark eyes dead with desperation. He pushed the door open on the passenger side and pulled me across the seat as he stepped out. I stumbled to my feet on the side of some road, having lost one of my high heels somewhere in the turbulence.

But that wasn't the worst of it.

The windshield was splattered with blood, and just under it, the driver was slumped over the steering wheel. I looked away as fast as I could.

Second time I'd seen a dead body in a little over a

week's time. What the hell had happened to my peaceful, boring life as an art student and teacher?

Another deafening gunshot rang out and Jorge pulled me down behind the side of the car.

"Let me go. Please, just let me go, Jorge," I begged.

He snickered. "My name's not Jorge, you dumb bitch. And shut your mouth."

Oh. *Tony*. Regardless, I wasn't giving up that easily. If there was one thing my father had taught me, it was that everyone has their price.

"Okay. Tony. My father's rich. He'll give you anything you want. No questions asked. Just let me go. And my sister, too—"

"SHUT UP," he bellowed, peeking around the car from our hiding place. "Shut your fucking mouth or I'll whack you so hard you won't have any teeth left to talk."

Another shot rang out and I crunched myself into the smallest ball I could, my hands still restrained behind me in cuffs.

"Fuckers," he spat, jumping up long enough to fire twice.

Under the streetlamp, there was enough light to see something dark soaked into the legs of my yellow jumpsuit.

The wet I'd felt on the floor of the car?
Blood.

CHAPTER 30

RAIN

Jesus, who were these people? And whose blood had been spilled recently enough for it to still be wet enough to soak into my clothes?

Another girl they'd kidnapped?

And why the blood? Had they killed her? Had she fought harder than I, knowing there was nobody to come for her?

After all, I had Nico.

"Let her go, fucker," Nico called from a distance.

Oh thank god.

He might not be able to get me out of the mess I was in, but at least he was trying. That would be of some comfort to my parents.

"Shit. Where's the other car?" Tony muttered.

He had another car coming? Christ, I was screwed.

These guys seemed to have no end of resources to get what they wanted.

That meant their network was vast. And powerful. And well-funded.

How many people were in on this? Were men and women like Tony and Francesca walking the streets of every city in the world, just looking for young women to grab?

"Hold it right there, Tony," a voice said from behind us.

"Colt. What the fuck are you doing, man? Put that goddamn gun down," Jorge/Tony said.

Colt was here? And how did he know Jorge was Tony?

My mind ping-ponged with the possibilities of where the moment was going to go. I knew I should have been thrilled Colt was on the scene, but if I'd learned anything the last few days, it was not to assume anything.

"Move away from her," Colt growled.

Tony released my arm with a shove and inched away.

"Guys," Colt called. "I got them. Over here."

I heard footsteps running toward us.

Out of the corner of my eye, I saw Tony spring to his feet. "Colt, I'm gonna kill you, you fucker—"

But Colt moved first, and with one last gunshot, Tony was propelled back against the car and then slumped to the ground.

The horror of what was happening rushed me all at once, and coupled with the adrenaline slamming through my veins, was more than I could take.

"Help me, Colt, please help me. Get these handcuffs off," I screamed, writhing and approaching a full-blown panic attack.

"Rain!" Nico shouted, pulling me to my feet with Dom right on his heels.

I slumped into him, howling with the fear of the last half hour, and the agony that my sister had gone through the same thing and not had the lucky outcome I had.

"Dom, get the key out of his pocket," Nico said.

He stroked my hair. "It's okay. I've got you. You're safe," he murmured in my ear.

Someone behind me fumbled with my handcuffs, and I was suddenly free.

But I was too wasted to even put my arms around Nico. I just let him half-carry me back to his car.

"Good work, Colt."

I stopped walking. I had to acknowledge the man who'd saved me. "Colt," I said, looking at him, "Thank you."

He looked at me briefly, then looked away. "You're welcome," he mumbled.

"Yeah, man, way to go," Dom called after him as he walked away.

I looked up at Nico. "What's up with him?"

He shrugged, watching Colt return to his car. "Don't know. Tired maybe."

It was never fun to shoot people, I supposed.

Dom jumped into the front seat of the car where Smitt was waiting, and Nico and I got in the back.

Nico took my trembling hands in his. "Did they hurt you?"

I took a deep breath. "No, they didn't. I might have a few bruises, and I'm covered in someone else's blood, but I'm fine."

At least on the outside. What wasn't okay were the visions of what my sister had gone through, since I'd had my own close call. All I could think about was how terrified she must have been, especially in the knowledge that no one knew where the hell she was being taken.

I looked up at Nico. "We *have* to find my sister. After tomorrow, my dad takes over. And I'm afraid that will push the operation further underground. My dad is not a delicate man. He will barge in like the bull that he is and turn everything upside down. And that might not be for the best."

"I know. I wasn't going to tell you, because I didn't want to get your hopes up, but Colt tells me he has a contact who knows where Mazzy is. She might still be in the country. We're trying to confirm."

I bolted upright. "What? Are you serious? Oh my god, that's amazing."

Hope filled me and my heart soared. I might see my little sister again.

Please, please, please…

Nico held a hand up. "Hold on. Don't get too excited. Just because we find out where she is, that does not guarantee we will be able to get to her."

My poor Mazzy.

"We'll do our goddamn best, I can promise you that. I want to find your sister as much as you do, especially since I've met your parents. But this isn't a done deal."

My momentary elation began to subside.

I put my head in my hands. I was living a nightmare. That's all there was to it.

"I'm sorry, Rain."

He continued in a lowered voice. "I'm sorry I forced you to make a deal with me. It was shitty. I don't know what I was thinking. I was just being a dick."

I put my hands on the sides of his face. He might not be a perfect man, but I would be in the hands of traffickers if not for him and his buddies.

Back at the compound, Smitt and Dom popped out of the car, and with a glance over their shoulders, left us alone, scanning the property, their hands on their weapons.

"Nico—"

"No, Rain, wait. I realized tonight, when I thought you might be gone for good, that I didn't know what I'd do without you. The shit show of my past came back.

I... couldn't live through another one. I'd be... destroyed."

Holy shit. This man bared his soul in a way I never thought he could.

"Yeah, so... I'm getting attached to you." He looked up at me. "Wait, scratch that. I *am* attached to you. Why be a pussy about it? I'm owning it."

He laughed, shaking his head.

These men didn't mess around.

I took Nico's face in both my hands. "You don't have to apologize. Thank you, I appreciate it, but you don't have to."

With one look, I knew he had my best interests at heart. And he *had* my heart, truth be told.

The question was, would that keep me safe, or find my sister?

CHAPTER 31

NICO

"This is heavenly," Rain purred, sinking deeper into the steaming bubble bath I'd run for her.

I propped myself on the edge of the tub and handed her the warm milk she'd asked for, hoping to take her mind off the events of the evening if just for a little while.

"Try and relax," I said, lighting a couple candles.

As soon as she'd closed her eyes, I scooped up her dirty, bloody clothing and took it to the kitchen garbage. No need for her to look at the mess any longer than necessary.

What a fucking night. Actually, what a fucking week.

And I didn't know whether to punch Colt or kiss him. He'd saved Rain by killing her abductor, but it was his fault she'd been taken in the first place. It would be awhile before I could trust him again.

Yeah, we'd been friends for years, even longer than we'd known Dom, but in recent history, Colt had been growing distant, like he needed a change or wanted out of our high stakes business. He was spending less and less time with Dom and me, and when he was with us, he was often a surly pain in the ass.

Which was okay, if that's how he needed to play it. I got that people burned out on shit like ours. If I were he, I might take my cash and go bum around the Caribbean for a couple years on a sailboat loaded with beautiful ladies.

That would cure whatever ailed him.

I made a mental note to check on him in the morning to see if he needed some sort of break. A vacation, maybe.

Hell, I wouldn't mind a break myself. Maybe when all was said and done with Rain and her sister, assuming the outcome was what we were all hoping for, I could take my girl someplace far away and exotic.

Yeah, I liked Rain. A lot. I wasn't going to lie about it. And if she felt the same way, well, I was going to nurture things as best I could. No more taking shit for granted and being inattentive to my partner. That hadn't worked out too well the first time around, as I'd learned the hard way. I didn't blame my ex for hitting the road. Any woman should have done the same.

Rain was like a second chance at life for me, one I

hadn't been waiting for, or ever expected. I figured I blew it the first time, and that was it. End of story. But the night she entered the elevator, shoes in hand and looking for all the world like she wanted to punch someone, I'd been hooked.

There was no denying it any longer.

Sure, she was beautiful and sexy. But what really got me was her quiet determination to make something of her life away from her dad's money and all the privilege it afforded her.

She wanted the satisfaction of knowing that the good things that came her way were a result of her hard work and talent.

And, judging by the interest in her one painting at this evening's fateful gallery show, she was on the right track.

I returned to help her out of the tub by wrapping a thick, white towel around her, and rubbing down her shoulders and arms with another. Fuck if she didn't smell great. She unpinned her hair and let it tumble down her back, and when the towel slipped, she looked just like Lady Godiva.

And my dick was getting harder by the second.

"C'mon, baby. Let's turn in."

I led her to bed and tucked her under the thick down comforter. I checked the room next door, where Smitt was standing guard. I closed the door between the two rooms quietly and crawled into bed myself.

I sidled up to Rain, who turned to face me and

pressed her lips to mine. After what she'd been through, she could still be tender. Her resilience amazed me.

She threw a leg over me, opening herself up. Her pussy was warm and wet, and begging for attention. I ran my fingers through her slick folds, and she shuddered, hopefully releasing some of the tension of the day.

I rolled her to her back and slipped between her thighs. In the dim room I could see her gaze locked with mine, and I realized the closeness I felt with her was entirely new for me.

Reaching, I grabbed a condom from my nightstand and sheathed myself with it. I was dying to feel her warm pussy directly on my cock, but if things went according to plan, there'd be time for that later.

I slipped inside, taking my time, and fuck if her walls didn't grip me like a vise. As I held myself above her, I took a deep breath to keep from exploding before we'd even gotten started.

"God, baby, you feel so good," I murmured.

"Oh, Nico. Please. I want more."

When I was all the way inside, I held myself there to experience the throbbing of her pussy. She responded with small gyrations of her hips, just enough to drive me wild.

I gritted my teeth. "Babe, I'm gonna come. I'm gonna come."

She put her hands on both sides of my face and pressed her forehead to mine.

"Give it to me, Nico. Fuck me," she breathed.

So I let go and my entire being shattered inside my girl. I'd never been so connected to anyone, much less a beauty like Rain. Not even my ex-wife.

We fell asleep minutes later, my arms wrapped around her to keep her safe.

CHAPTER 32

NICO

SOMEONE WAS SHAKING ME. I looked around the dark room, unsure how long I'd been asleep, and found Rain holding the covers up to her chin, her eyes wide with terror.

"Babe, what's wrong—"

She looked at me, directing my gaze to the end of the bed.

I squinted in the dark. What the hell was Colt doing there, in my bedroom, in the middle of the night?

"That's who was watching me the other night. When you had to go to work. I'd thought it was Dom," Rain whispered in a shaky voice.

What the fuck?

"Hey, buddy," I said to Colt, squinting in the dark to try to make out his expression. Something about him said to tread carefully. "What's up? What are you doing here?"

I sat up to swing my legs over the side of the bed and grab my boxers.

"Stop right there," he growled.

But I slowly reached to flick my nightstand's light on. When I did, I saw Colt standing there in his clothes from the night before, holding a gun on us.

What the hell? I was still clearing the sleep from my head, but even if I hadn't been, I'd still be fucking confused.

"I told you not to move."

I put my hands up to show I was complying. "Just turning on the light, Colt. I wanted to see what the hell was going on."

"*Fuck you,*" he said.

Okayyyy… And where was Smitt? Our doors had been locked when I'd last checked.

"Colt, would you please tell me what's up? Why are you here and what do you want? Look, you're scaring the shit out of Rain here. Can we take this outside and talk about it?"

I had to stall for time—going from sound asleep to high alert took a moment. I needed to get my thoughts straight.

Colt didn't give a shit about that.

"Shut up, asshole," he said.

He turned his attention to Rain, staring her down with an ugly, menacing face.

She reached across the bed, searching for my hand.

"Colt, can we just get dressed? We'll have a glass of scotch and you can tell me what's on your mind."

I wanted to get him as far away from Rain as possible. There was something in the way he was looking at her that raised the hairs on the back of my neck, and from the look on her face, she sensed something bad was up, too.

But *Colt?* We'd been friends all our lives. We'd run a dozen businesses together and had always pretty much gotten along like brothers. Yeah, we disagreed from time to time and got pissed at each other, but at the end of the day, we always saw things the same way. We always ended up on the same page.

Maybe those days were over?

"You always get what you want, don't you?" He snickered, narrowing his eyes.

Okay. He was clearly not in his right mind. It was time to negotiate. Carefully.

I shrugged to appease him, hoping my body language appeared to give him the upper hand. "Look, man. I'm not sure what you're going on about. But I want to help you. I really do—"

"Fuck off. You've never cared about anyone but yourself," he spat, the gun in his hand moving from me to Rain and back.

Christ. Had he felt that way all these years, and was now overflowing with a lifetime of resentment and rage?

That was some scary shit, the kind that could make a man go crazy.

"All right. All right, Colt. What's going on? Talk to me."

He turned to Rain and gestured with his chin. "Get up. Get dressed."

She looked at me, confused. I knew she wanted to know what was going on, too, but with a gun pointed at her, there wasn't much chance of discussion.

Rain swung her feet over the edge of the bed, keeping a tight hold on the duvet cover for modesty.

"All my clothes are in the cottage," she said quietly.

"Nico. Go get her some sweats. Hurry up."

I slipped into the boxer shorts I'd left by the bed, and slowly walked to my closet, taking a quick mental inventory of any weapons I had stored there.

"If you pull anything, I'll put a bullet in her head," he snarled.

I searched through my dresser drawers as if I were looking for something to give Rain to wear. In reality, I was buying time to decide if I could pull off loading the gun I had stored in my closet and taking down Colt.

The thought horrified me. Taking down my friend? But he'd threatened Rain.

And that was going a step too far.

"Here," I said, throwing some clothes on the bed for Rain to put on. "Seriously, Colt. What the hell are you doing? Were you the one behind the security breaches?

Was it one of your guys who murdered Clare and almost got Rain?"

Like a fog lifting, things were becoming clear. Why he'd let Rain leave the gallery with a stranger, why he'd made sure the guard house was unattended... it was all starting to make sense.

Sad, fucked-up sense.

Who else did he have on his payroll?

He watched Rain, who'd turned her back to him, get dressed.

"Colt, don't take her. Don't do this. We've been friends all our lives. Please."

He looked at me with dark, empty eyes. It was like the man I'd known nearly all my life had died and was inhabited by some ugly, tortured soul.

"Please, Colt. I love her."

At that, both Colt's and Rain's heads whipped in my direction. Then Colt dropped his head back, and let out a loud cackle.

"Good. Then that means you can spend the rest of your life wondering what happened to her and which wealthy Middle Eastern prince made a concubine out of her for himself and his friends."

Fucker. He was going to die. If not that night, then another. I'd be after him until the end of my days, if necessary.

A sob escaped Rain's lips as she dropped the clothes she was trying to put on.

"Don't go, Rain," I said. As if she had a choice.

She shook her head frantically. "If it means I'll see my sister, I'll go. Colt, please just make sure I get to see my sister."

"Fuck you and your sister. You pretty girls are all alike, thinking you're above the shit sandwiches life throws around. Well, now you're learning. And I'll be richer than god when they get a load of you. They're not gonna fucking believe the jackpot they hit with this one. Get dressed!"

He turned back to me. "And I'll never have to see *your* fucking face again as long as I live."

He couldn't take her. He couldn't. She meant everything to me.

But for the first time in my life, I was at a loss. He was taking away the one thing he knew was important to me.

What the hell had I done to him? Had it been that bad?

"Colt, you know you won't get away with this. Don't do it."

He grabbed Rain by the upper arm and dragged her across the room toward the door.

I lunged, but before I could reach him, something cold and hard blindsided me and hit my temple. As I sank to the floor, I wondered what the warm, sticky substance was running down the side of my face.

Then, everything went black.

CHAPTER 33

RAIN

"I THOUGHT YOU WERE MY FRIEND."

Colt cackled like a crazy man. "I *am* your friend. And you are mine. *And*, you are about to do me a big, huge favor that will pay off in spades. In fact, thank you in advance."

Jesus. The cruelty.

He looked at me with his shit-eating grin and doubled down. "I really appreciate it, Rain."

If there hadn't been someone in the backseat of the car with a gun pointed at my head, I would have killed Colt with my bare hands.

"Where are we going?"

"*You* are leaving the country. I am leaving town as soon as I drop you off, to find another target-rich environment. It's all so perfect, isn't it? You ladies are out there, ripe for the picking. I'm shuttling women out of the country left and right, and Nico and Dom thought all along that I was trying to save them. Ridiculous hero syndrome, that's what I call it. Like they can fight these networks. It's fruitless. They'll never win. That's why I joined them. Well, that, and the money."

"You're sick, Colt. You're a sick man."

He waved my comment off like it was an annoying gnat. "Oh, and don't worry, you don't need your passport or ID in case you were thinking lack of either would protect you from leaving. We have an entire system for moving girls like you around." He glanced over at me. "Look on the bright side. You don't have to go through airport security ever again. Now that's a bonus if you ask me."

He chuckled.

Had Nico known his friend was such a psycho?

A few resigned tears dribbled down my face, and I leaned my head against the cool passenger door window at an utter loss over what to do.

There wasn't anything I *could* do. Was there? Not for myself and not for my sister.

This was going to kill my parents. Losing both daughters? As if one weren't bad enough.

And my dad was going to murder Nico. He'd be on the receiving end of a fury the likes of which he'd never seen. And knowing Nico, he'd take the punishment headed his way. He'd failed my sister, and he'd failed me, though not through any fault of his own. God knew he tried his best. He just didn't know the evil he was looking for was right under his nose. In his own house, essentially.

His best friend from childhood turning on him? What a devastating betrayal.

So. No more Vegas. No more LA. No more United States, I supposed.

And certainly no more Nico.

I turned to Colt, whose driving was getting erratic. "Colt, if you are part of this whole operation, why did you shoot the guy who grabbed me at the gallery last night?"

He shrugged. "Oh, that loser? It was clear he wasn't going to get away with you, so I had to make it look like I was on your side until I had my own opportunity to grab you. Like I did this morning. You guys looked so peaceful sleeping. I almost hated to break it up. Christ, I haven't seen Nico that happy in years. Poor bastard." He shook his head.

I studied his profile, which I'd once thought so handsome. Now all I could see was ugly hate. Had it been there all along and I'd just not recognized it? I guess you see what you want to. I needed these guys to protect me, so I'd looked at them as heroes. Knights in shining armor.

Yeah, right.

"Why did you, then, wake us up to take me away?" I asked.

"Are you kidding? Darling, you know how much

goddamn money a girl like you is worth? I'm talking millions when all is said and done. You're making me a rich man."

Maybe I could play on his sympathies? "What about what that means for me?"

He got on the freeway, driving way too fast. "Well, that's what I call collateral damage. It's a shame, but someone has to be sacrificed. And today is your turn."

Okay, he had no sympathy. But there was the money angle...

"Look, Colt," I said, turning to him as he drove even faster toward North Las Vegas. "My dad is rich. He will give you the millions you want. And, if you can get my sister back to us, he'll give you even more. He'll give you everything he has."

Even his life. I knew how my dad was.

"Well, that's a great idea, but no can do. I'm committed to a huge network. If I don't bring in some worthwhile goods, not only do I not get paid, I also get my head shot off. It's very motivating," he said, nodding.

God, he was fucking crazy.

"Why are you doing this? Didn't you like being in business with Dom and Nico? You guys seemed to make a lot of money together with your investments and... other stuff."

The compound where they lived cost a pretty penny, no doubt. I'd been around wealth all my life, and

I could easily see those guys were far from broke. On the contrary, they lived pretty damn well.

"Yeah, I get that. But I'm ready for serious fucking money. Like *buy an island* kind of money." He stole a glance at me. "Your old man doesn't have that kind of dough. Sorry, baby. Very few people do. That's why I love doing business with the Saudi princes. Now, those are some rich mother fuckers."

I'd known the night before when Nico brought me home that we weren't at the end of the bullshit. And I'd been right. I just knew that somehow, someday, I'd be right back where I was, being dragged into the unknown by some bastard out to make a buck.

It was over. All of it. Someone had cracked open Nico's skull, and Smitt and possibly Dom were either killed or at least incapacitated. Nico could be dead too, for all I knew.

The lump in my throat built, but I did my best to swallow it away. I would not cry in front of this man.

No one was coming for me this time. There was no one. I was alone. Completely fucking alone.

It must have been exactly how Mazzy had felt when she was being dragged off.

Had it been a blessing or a curse to have met Nico? On one hand, I never would have known what had happened to my sister if he hadn't found out for me. It would have been as if she'd vanished into thin air.

But on the other hand, would the traffickers have come for me, had they not found me through him?

Either way, I was screwed. There was no happy outcome.

And even though it had been preceded by a terrifying experience, my last night with Nico had been magical. His care was evident in his every action, from my candlelit bath to our slow lovemaking.

I'd never had a man like him in my life. And I would not have another.

That thought loosened the sobs that had been backed up in my throat, and I put my head in my hands, shaking. Pride be damned, Colt was going to witness my despair.

Why did this happen? And for what good?

Nothing made sense.

"What did you do with Smitt and Dom?" I asked in a trembling voice.

Colt gestured toward the backseat. "Ask him."

I started to turn around but a gun poked my shoulder.

"Keep facing front. And don't worry about those guys. They're none of your business," the man in back growled.

Colt whipped around a corner and pulled the car into the North Las Vegas airport where we parked in a small, private hangar. A large garage door closed behind us, and I blinked to adjust to the harsh fluorescent light.

"Okay," he said. "Let's get this party started."

Hopping out of the car, he hurried around to the passenger side and opened the door, waving me out.

"Let's go. We gotta get you cleaned up."

When I hesitated, he yanked me so hard I stumbled. "Get up!" he screamed, bending in my face.

Every fiber of my being was so overloaded with fear, all I could do was put one foot in front of the other. I wasn't capable of much more.

It was like a death march.

With Colt gripping my arm, we passed a series of offices where a couple women were busily at work. They paid us no attention. None at all.

Did they see women like me dragged through the premises all the time? Was this just another day at the office for these ladies?

Colt pushed me into a room with a few folding chairs, a rack of hanging dresses, and a box of old clothing and shoes. He pointed toward a bathroom.

"Clean yourself up and get dressed in something nice. We can't bring you anywhere looking like a homeless person." He looked me up and down in disgust.

I stood there, unable to move, like in one of those nightmares where you're watching yourself go through something horrible but you can't wake up.

"Yeah, a pretty blonde like you is gonna fetch a handsome sum," he salivated.

I looked around the room. There had to be a way out.

But no. There wasn't even a single fucking window. The only way out was the way I'd come in—the doorway where Colt stood, and through the hallway past where people were working.

I was going to be sick.

"Could I have some water?" I managed to whisper.

"Have all the water you want. The bathroom's right there. Now get in the shower and clean up and then put one of those nice dresses on." He slammed the door, locking me in.

I gulped water from a grimy sink until my stomach calmed and stepped in the shower once I'd tied my hair into a knot on top of my head. There was only one bath towel that hadn't been washed in god knew how long, so I stood dripping and shivering while I wiped myself down with paper towels.

I bundled Nico's sweats into my arms and nearly fell to my knees in anguish when I realized how much they smelled like him—nothing fancy, but basic, clean man.

I didn't even know if he were alive.

But I couldn't think about that just then. I had to keep my wits about me. I had to survive.

I flipped through the dresses on the rack. Christ, it was an odd time to be selective about clothing. I chose the ugliest thing I could find, hoping that it would somehow make me less desirable.

Once I'd zipped myself into the poorly fitting dress, an old turquoise-y bridesmaid number, I dug through the box of shoes, burrowing all the way to the bottom to find a match for the silver pump I'd managed to squeeze my right foot into. As I did, something purple and shiny at the bottom of the box caught my eye.

Reaching through the tangle of heels, I tugged at it, but no luck.

So I started flinging shoes out of the box, littering the floor. I glanced over my shoulder. No Colt, at least not yet.

When I'd cleared a path, I got a grip on a piece of stretchy fabric and pulled hard. Now free, it sprang from the box and snapped into the shape of a little party dress, the kind young women wear to clubs and such, so short they pull on the hem all night and still barely remain covered.

It was the kind of dress my sister Mazzy had been wearing the last night I'd seen her.

In fact, it *was* Mazzy's dress. I could smell her perfume on it.

I buried my face in it and tears threatened again. But I fought them.

Now was not the time.

Mazzy had been here. And it broke my fucking heart

I bunched the dress into as small a bundle as I could, as if it were as close as I'd ever get to her again. I held it to my chest and could actually feel pain in my heart.

What else might be in the box? I tore through it, looking.

How about a fully charged cell phone and a loaded gun? Or a Swiss army knife? Was that too much to ask?

Apparently so, because I didn't turn up a damn thing.

But there were two sharp objects that, if wielded carefully, could inflict some harm.

The shoes on my feet.

Whoever was in charge of this operation had failed to realize how deadly a stiletto could be. I was basically wearing two five-inch daggers. If I played my cards right, they might just come in handy.

And if they were to come in handy, I'd have to figure out how, pretty fucking fast. Footsteps neared the locked door, and in a second, Colt burst in.

He looked me over with a smirk. "Ugly dress. Ouch. Well, this will have to do for now. Are you ready?"

"Ready for what?" I asked, still clinging to Mazzy's dress.

"Ready to meet your new owner."

CHAPTER 34

NICO

WHOEVER HAD CRACKED me over the head was an amateur thug, because, while he broke the skin that resulted in a nice, bloody mess, he'd left me with little more than a mild headache.

Thank god.

I wanted to check on Smitt and Dom—god knew what Colt might have done with them. But Rain was my priority at the moment.

I had to save her. At any cost.

Even if it meant the lives of my friends.

I grabbed my motorcycle helmet as I ran out of the house to get my FZ1 Yamaha. That baby would fly, allowing me to slalom through the shitty Vegas traffic that would certainly hold up any vehicle with four wheels. I put the bike in gear and headed north.

MIKA LANE

Did I know with certainty that was where they'd taken Rain? No, but if they needed to get her out of the country ASAP, like they always did with new girls, that was the only place large enough for a private plane to land.

Fuckers. And that Colt. Bastard was going to pay.

As I raced in between cars on the freeway—which was highly illegal in Nevada—I tried to keep my head clear to focus on my driving. Riding a bike wasn't for the faint of heart, and racing like a bat out of hell increased the inherent dangers to an exponential degree.

I couldn't help but think of my Rain—yeah, that's how I thought of her now—under me last night as I fucked her into oblivion.

What if it was the last time I got to be with her?

One thought about those trafficking pigs putting their hands on her, and I opened the bike to almost one hundred mph. It was dangerous as hell—I could go to jail for speeding like that, but a police encounter was the least of my worries.

I'd lost a woman I'd loved before. It was my own damn fault, I'd be the first to admit it, but it had leveled me for years. Just when I was crawling back out of my cave, Rain had come along.

And just as quickly, she was gone.

I'd promised myself I'd do things differently this time. No more being a disinterested and neglectful asshole. When I was married, I'd buried myself in work, as my family had expected of me. I never imagined that could mean losing the most important thing in my life.

And as if my wife leaving wasn't bad enough, what was even worse was *who* she'd left me *for*.

My brother.

No shit.

My wife left me for my brother.

As soon as I'd found out, I'd never spoken to either of them again. Couldn't even tell you if they were dead or alive.

That was pretty much how I ended up in Vegas. My business partner, Leo, was coming back here from New York, and I figured what the hell. Try out the desert. How bad could it be?

It's a dry heat, everyone will tell you.

It was true, that it was dry, but it was also a miserable heat. And yet, there was something about it I still liked. Vegas was so unselfconscious compared to New York. It didn't have to prove anything to anyone. It was confidently unique, as if it knew no one could ever take that away.

I got a kick out of it.

My wife and I had been on the rocks for a while. I was at work all the time, and when I wasn't, I didn't hang out with her. Big mistake. You don't pull shit like that with today's women. It wasn't like it was in my dad's time, taking your partner for granted. I learned that the hard way. And I'd never do that again.

I'd never do it again if I were given the chance to start over, that is. And with the way things were going, I wasn't feeling hopeful. But I could give it my best shot.

Speaking of shots, the first one I fired would go right through Colt's head if I had anything to say about it. He'd always been a slimy fucker, but I'd put up with him because we had so much history. He was the kind of guy who, when we were kids, lied about every fucking thing just for the sake of lying. I'd thought it was funny at the time, because he got us out of a lot of scrapes, but looking back, I could see it was pathological.

I just couldn't believe he'd so totally turned against me. It was bad enough he'd gotten wrapped up in trafficking. What kind of sick fuck does that? And then, to make off with my girl? Did he really hate me that much?

Apparently, so.

It explained his strange behavior of late, including letting Rain walk out the door at the gallery with a total stranger.

I forced myself to take deep breaths as the airport tower came into view. It wouldn't do anybody any good were I to do something stupid and get myself killed. Even if I couldn't save Rain and her sister this time, I'd spend the rest of my life looking for them. I needed to stay alive.

I slowed to quiet the bike as I approached the small

airport. There were several large hangars, and I could see the far one where trucks were shuttling back and forth, getting a private jet ready for a trip.

They were the kind of trucks that prepare a jet for a *long* trip. Like an over the ocean trip.

Jesus. I'd gotten there just in time.

I left my bike behind the hangar and silently moved around the side, my gun drawn and ready. I wasn't sure what I was going to find but there was one thing I was sure of—that Colt wasn't in there alone, and that the folks who *were* in there, were most likely armed and ready for somebody like me to come along and try to interfere with their plans.

As I neared the door, I kept my back pressed against the corrugated steel exterior of the building. It was relatively quiet, with only sounds of mechanics preparing the plane to fly.

Just then, my phone vibrated with a text.

From Smitt.

I breathed a sign of relief.

thought you were dead

no such luck. i'm with dom. where are you?

NLV airport. hangar 3

i knew it. we're on our way. colt there?

not sure yet. how close are you?

ten mins

CHAPTER 35

NICO

WELL, I'd be damned. My friends weren't dead. If they'd been knocked on the head like I had, they probably had headaches and were bloody, but were none the worse for wear. I looked at my watch. If I could scope out the place before they arrived, we might be able to take them by surprise.

Finally, I heard some voices.

"How many you have for this trip?" someone asked.

"Just a couple. But they're good. Real good. Like gold good."

Holy fuck, that was Colt. By that point I knew he was in on the trafficking, but to hear him talk about it so nonchalantly was a gut punch.

Colt, what happened to you, man?

"How much longer? I want you guys to get out of here. I gotta hit the road, too," he said.

"Mmm. Not sure. The pilot's in the cockpit doing his thing, and the copilot is on his way. So where're you taking off to after the plane leaves?"

"I think I'll hit the road for Mexico and lie low for a while. Then, see who I can meet down there to help build the network. Might be some tough competition, though," Colt said.

"Oh yeah. I hear the Mexican program is pretty well established."

"Right. I hear ya. In any case, there should be some way to partner. A very lucrative way to partner."

Both of them laughed. And I was dying to take their heads off.

The callous way they talked about abducting women for their own pocketbooks. I hadn't been the most honorable business person all my life, but I'd never gotten involved in shit like that. I couldn't fathom it.

My phone buzzed.

we're here

drive around behind the hangars and leave your car where you see my bike. come around on the left side of the building. i'm on the right side

will do

I heard Smitt's car quietly crunching gravel and then stop. Colt and his team must have really thought they'd killed us or at least taken us out for the long term with the casual way they were chatting. They didn't suspect a thing.

Or maybe they were always on their guard.

I knew Colt had incredible reflexes. If he even had a hint that we were closing in, the fight would be tough. The only way to overpower him was with the advantage of surprise.

So Colt was good. But so were Smitt and Dom.

That's when I heard high heels clicking over the hangar's concrete floor. My pulse started to race—was that Rain? Was she okay?

But I didn't need to wonder for long. "Colt, please. Please don't do this. I told you, my father will pay you more than anyone else."

I heard Rain stumble as Colt growled, "Get going. And shut up."

She choked back a sob.

ready?

yup

on the count of three...

Three...

Two...

One...

"Let her go, you fucker," I hollered as I whipped around the corner and trained my gun on my old friend.

Colt jerked around, drawing his own weapon. The surprise in his face was evident, and for a moment he released Rain. She started to run, but in her high heels, she didn't get far before she slipped on the slick concrete floor.

"Rain, stay down!" Dom shouted.

He turned toward the front of the plane and fired right through the cockpit window.

They weren't going anywhere now.

Two women emerged from the office, and when they saw what was going on, screamed and ran back in. The man Colt had been talking to also ran for the office.

"Stop right there," Dom shouted.

The man reached for his gun and turned, but Dom got him first. He sank to the ground with a bullet to the chest.

"Smitt, get the women," I called, "and check for weapons."

Colt made a dash for the plane's stairs.

"Don't Colt. Don't run. Please," Dom called, training his gun on him just as I had.

"Fuck you both," he screamed, firing as he backed up the steps.

But he only got one shot off before Dom—or was it I?—got him first.

We'd never know.

Colt slumped over then slid back down the steps he'd just ascended.

Rain was in my arms in seconds as Dom ran to check Colt's condition.

He looked at me with tears in his eyes, shaking his head.

Our friend from childhood was dead.

"Oh god," Rain cried, burying her head in my chest.

We still didn't know if there was anyone armed on the plane. I pulled Rain over behind a steel cabinet.

"Stay here. Don't come out until I tell you."

Dom was already at the top of the steps, waiting for me.

He leaned against the outside of the plane. "If anybody's in there, now's your chance to come out alive," he hollered through the open door.

Nothing.

"Cover me, buddy," he said, and ducked inside.

"Holy shit," I heard him say moments later.

I ran in, and at first, didn't see him. But when I looked to the rear of the plane, I found him towering over a woman who was scrunched into a corner.

She pulled her limbs into a tighter ball and tucked her head, terrified.

She looked like Rain. Certainly close enough to be a sister.

"Are you Mazzy?" I asked.

"Yes," she whispered, looking up with wide eyes.

Dom crouched in front of her. "Is there anyone else on the plane?" he asked.

"The pilot. But there was a gunshot."

I reached my hand out. "Mazzy, we're here to help.

And there's someone here who wants to see you very badly."

Her gaze snapped up at me, and she looked at Dom. He nodded.

"Mazzy, you're safe now."

She took my hand and slowly rose to her feet. She wore an evening dress and high heels, but her arms were covered in bruises.

I prayed nothing worse had been done to her.

I guided her to the door, and we stepped out and down the stairs.

"Rain. There's someone here you might want to see," I called.

She poked her head from around the cabinet where she was hiding. When she saw Mazzy, she fell to her knees, crying.

"Oh my god, Mazzy, it's you." She looked up with a tear-stained face, unable to move.

But Mazzy screamed and ran to her sister, throwing her arms around her so hard the two toppled over, laughing and crying at the same time.

"Damn. That's what I call a good day at the office," Dom said, beaming.

CHAPTER 36

RAIN

STILL CLINGING TO EACH OTHER, Mazzy and I somehow managed to get back on our feet.

"Ladies, I know you're having a happy reunion, but we have to get out of here. Others will be arriving at any moment."

Mazzy and I both chucked the high heels we'd been wearing, and we ran with Dom and Nico around the side of the airplane hangar.

"Where's Smitt?" I asked.

"Right there," Dom said, pointing to him sitting behind the wheel of the car.

That guy was always one step ahead.

Mazzy and I piled into the backseat, and when Nico didn't follow, I turned to see him starting his motorcycle and putting his helmet on.

I gave him a little wave, wishing I'd had the chance to kiss him.

Before Dom's door was even shut, Smitt took off, skidding through the parking lot gravel, and back to the freeway. Nico was just behind us, and as soon as we hit the pavement, he waved and took off.

And looked very hot doing so, I might add.

"Smitt, what happened to the ladies working in the office?" I asked.

"Locked 'em up in a back room. Someone will find them eventually," he laughed.

The back room, where I'd found Mazzy's dress.

My sister held my hand with a death grip.

"Mazzy, where have you been? We thought maybe they'd taken you out of the country or something."

"I was there at the airplane hangar. There are rooms above the offices. Those ladies you saw live there. I guess they look after the girls before they get shipped out."

We shivered in disgust.

"Thank god you came, Rain. I'd given up hope. I thought I'd never see you again."

That was when Mazzy's sobs got hard and loud. I held her and stroked her hair through my own tears.

"Can I have someone's phone? We have to call our parents."

Dom passed his over the backseat, and I let Mazzy do the honors.

In seconds of her dialing, there were more tears, and not a few shrieks from the other end of the line.

My sister babbled to my parents, and while I was pretty sure they could make little or no sense of the story she was trying to tell, they were nonetheless thrilled to hear from her.

"Here, Dad wants to talk to you," a sniffling Mazzy said, handing me the phone.

I couldn't wait to hear his voice. "Hi, Dad. Can you believe it?"

"Well, your friend Nico really came through."

He didn't know the half of it.

"Yup. He's good that way. Dad, we'll be home as soon as we can get there. We can't wait to see you and Mom."

I said my goodbyes as we pulled into the compound. Off to the left of the property stood Colt's house, and a pang of sadness swept through me. How did someone get pulled so far off track that he betrayed his childhood friends, not to mention himself?

And now he was dead. I hated what he tried to do to my sister and me, but I also felt for him and the way he didn't appreciate the gift that friendships offer. What a loss. And a waste.

"Look at this place," Mazzy breathed as we pulled into the crushed stone driveway.

Nico's motorcycle sat in front of my cottage. He'd left us in the dust, that was how fast he rode.

Jumping out of the car as soon as it stopped, I ran and threw my arms around him.

"I don't know how to thank you," I said, kissing his face everywhere I possibly could.

"Okay, okay," he said, laughing. "Why don't you and your sister get cleaned up and we'll head to LA."

"Oh god, Nico. You are such an amazing man. How did you know that's just what I needed?"

"When I told your dad I was going to take care of business, I wasn't kidding. I want to show him I'm a man of my word and that I can make shit happen."

Well.

"And why are you suddenly so interested in impressing him?" I asked with a sly smile.

"Because now that I've done something for him, I want him to do something for me."

Why was he talking in riddles?

I squinted my eyes at Nico. "Are you saying what I think you're saying?"

He grinned. "If you're thinking that I want your father's blessing for you and me to start a life together, then you're right."

I couldn't stop smiling. "Well, what about what I want?" I teased.

"You'll have everything you want. For the rest of your life."

I had a feeling he was right.

EPILOGUE

It wasn't until I saw my parents in person that I realized just how horrifying the whole experience of Mazzy's being missing had been for them. And we'd decided we wouldn't even tell them about what had happened to me. I was afraid it would just push them over the edge.

As it was, when we got to their house, they both fell to their knees crying as soon as they saw Mazzy. And when we saw that, she and I were crying again, too.

Even Nico was wiping his eyes. My darling Nico. He saved my life. And he saved my sister's.

The rascal.

At first he'd made me come with him. Then he'd made me love him.

How could I not?

He was handsome, sexy, protective, smart, and best of all, he got me. He appreciated my goals and supported them. And he wanted me to paint, not only because that was what I loved, but also because he thought I was good.

In fact, after the dust had settled from Mazzy's ordeal, he approached me with an idea he'd probably had brewing for a while.

He wanted to open a gallery for me in Vegas, and if things went well there, open one in the more competitive market of Los Angeles.

I told him I was a long way from being ready for something like that, but it was lovely to have someone believe in me so deeply.

And to think it all started over a filthy little deal.

Did you like *Filthy Deal?*
Learn about the next book in the Dirty Games Series,
Foolish Dare

I hope you loved reading this book as much as I loved writing it. Please visit my store to learn more about my books, and to buy directly from me!
https://mikalaneshop.com/

ABOUT THE AUTHOR

Dear Reader:

I'm USA TODAY bestselling romance author Mika Lane, and am OBSESSED with bringing you sassy, steamy stories with imperfect heroines and the bad-a*s dudes they bring to their knees. I'll always bring you my signature humor and heat, topped off with a modern-day happily ever after.

My first book ever was *The Day I Ate the Milkyway,* a true fourth-grade masterpiece illustrated with crayons and bound with construction paper and glue. Nowadays, steamy romance gives purpose to my days and nights as I create worlds and characters that tickle the imagination. I live in magical Northern California with my own handsome alpha dude, sometimes known as Mr. Mika Lane, and two devilish cats named Chuck and Murray.

A dual citizen of the United States and Ireland, I have on more than one occasion spent my last dollar on a plane ticket somewhere, and am always planning my next escape. I often try new recipes on unsuspecting friends, search out hiding places to read undisturbed, and sadly kill every houseplant I bring home.

I LOVE to hear from readers when I'm not dreaming up naughty tales to share. Visit my online shop https:// mikalaneshop.com/ and say hello https:// mikalaneshop.com/pages/meet-mika.

xoxo, Mika